Donata's brain seemed to force-feed her sexual suggestions

She saw disjointed images of herself undressing Sean, of them entwined together on the fold-out sofa that lay not five feet away, of Sean's hands wrapping lengths of leather around her too-hot body....

Abruptly she stood. "I'd better go."

"Wait." His hand barely grazed the fabric of her angora sweater.

"I can't." She couldn't be around him when she felt so keyed up.

But then the light touch on her shoulder turned into a gentle stroke of her cheek and her knees nearly melted underneath her.

"Please." That one word held her in place, captive to whatever he might say. She tried not to breathe in his musky male scent for fear she'd end up returning the favor of his touch.

She'd been so intent on turning her life around that she'd kept her body, her heart and her feelings under lock and key. And although her heart seemed content to stay there, her body was making a hell of a case to be free....

Blaze™

Dear Reader,

Thank you for joining me this month for the debut of the NIGHT EYES miniseries, where danger and seduction meet and someone's always watching. For fans of my WEST SIDE CONFIDENTIAL series, *Don't Look Back* picks up at the NYPD's Tenth Precinct for a sexy and suspenseful adventure. You might recognize the bad-girl heroine, who's trying hard to reform—a task that's complicated when she crosses paths with P.I. Sean Beringer.

But if you haven't read the WEST SIDE CONFIDENTIAL stories, I think you'll enjoy this investigation turned steamy just the same! I hope you'll join me next month as NIGHT EYES continues with *Just One Look,* when we catch up with expert ballistics analyst Warren Vitalis, who finds himself at odds with a too-hot-to-handle divorcée who's running for her life.

Happy reading!

Joanne Rock

DON'T LOOK BACK
Joanne Rock

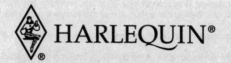

TORONTO • NEW YORK • LONDON
AMSTERDAM • PARIS • SYDNEY • HAMBURG
STOCKHOLM • ATHENS • TOKYO • MILAN • MADRID
PRAGUE • WARSAW • BUDAPEST • AUCKLAND

ISBN-13: 978-0-373-79309-9
ISBN-10:   0-373-79309-X

DON'T LOOK BACK

www.eHarlequin.com

Printed in U.S.A.

ABOUT THE AUTHOR

From *To Catch a Thief* to *Body Heat* and *The Big Easy*, RITA® Award-nominated author Joanne Rock loves a sexy suspense story where the hero and heroine aren't quite sure how far to trust one another. Her thirst for writing a wide range of stories has revisited this theme in both modern and medieval books alike. Her books have been reprinted in twenty-two countries and translated into sixteen languages. A former college teacher and public relations coordinator, she has a master's degree in English from the University of Louisville and started writing when she became a stay-at-home mom. Learn more about Joanne and her work by visiting her at www.joannerock.com.

Books by Joanne Rock

For Brenda Chin, who gave me that all-important first chance. Thank you for your guidance and support, and for expertly reading my story pitch over my shoulder when I couldn't seem to get the words out of my mouth. Six years after that first call, this is still the coolest job imaginable.

1

"I'm NOT WATCHING this with you."

Detective Donata Casale tossed the DVD case on the table in the 10th precinct's media room and glared at her so-called partner.

"Fine." Mick Juarez dumped a steady stream of sugar into his coffee and shrugged with the blasé confidence of a man who didn't have anything to prove. "Don't do your job. It's no skin off my nose."

The scent of java mixed with the stale stench of sweat and crime and cheap aftershave that permeated the building most days.

"Do you ever disagree with anyone about anything?" Donata resented Mick for his refusal to get riled up over stuff when life seemed hell-bent on pissing her off at every turn. "Doesn't it irritate you to know I got stuck with the porno case just because I'm new on the force and a woman?"

She picked up the DVD sleeve again and wondered why her lieutenant thought it would be a good idea to give the sex footage to her and Mick to watch when they were one of the few mixed-gender detective partnerships in the precinct's detective squad. Thankfully, at least Mick had sworn off women after his ex-wife did a number on him a few years back, so Donata never had to worry about any guy-girl chemistry getting in the way of a solid partnership.

"Maybe we got it because our past investigative work might connect to this somehow." Mick stirred his coffee for so long Donata thought she'd scream if he banged the spoon against the mug one more time. "Or maybe we had the lightest caseload to take on something new. Who knows? But to answer your question, no, it doesn't irritate me to be handed an important assignment."

Gently, he pried the DVD cover from her hand and Donata wondered how he could deflate her well-deserved fury so readily. The guy might have a serious sugar habit, but he was a rock. At thirty-eight, he was one of the most respected detectives on the squad. Patient and smart, Mick had outlasted four other partners to end up with her—the rookie no one else wanted because of her checkered past.

She might have been promoted quickly based on job performance, but in her years as a patrol officer, she'd seen the way cops could close ranks against outsiders. She'd overcome some of that bias in her last precinct, but then her promotion to detective had moved her to a new squad and put her at the back of the class all over again at the age of twenty-seven.

"Fine." Donata dropped into a chair near the computer screen and opened the file folder that had been given to them along with the DVD of an underage girl allegedly filmed without her knowledge. "But I'm closing my eyes during the naked parts. I really fail to see how us watching cheap porn will lead to finding any clues about a shady film distributor. From what I understand, the producers usually operate far away from the site of any actual studio humping."

Disgruntled to have been given an assignment surely intended to embarrass her, Donata studied the reports in the file while Mick clicked the necessary commands to load the video footage. New York's lower West Side might be home to a new adult filmmaker, but to her way of thinking, cops had more violent criminals to track than the lowlifes shipping porn across state lines. Possibly they could help a few mildly underage girls leave the business though, and at least that was a goal Donata could get behind. Then maybe watching this with Mick wouldn't feel like such a punishment.

"Maybe. Maybe not," Mick pointed out in typical unflappable fashion. "But one thing's for sure, lady, you've got to get over thinking the whole precinct is out to get you."

Donata stiffened, surprised even easygoing Mick would tread those waters.

She'd been about to remind him of a few choice comments their fellow officers had made the first day she'd been promoted to the detective squad two months ago, when a sudden outburst of profanity halted her.

Shocked at the uncharacteristic response from her partner, Donata looked up from the file notes to see a girl—fifteen at the oldest—slowly undoing her blouse in what appeared to be her home bedroom. Stuffed animals and posters of screen idols competed for space around her bed while the dim light of her computer screen provided the only illumination for her room.

"What the hell is this?" Mick stood so fast the rolling chair went flying out from underneath him as he thundered away from the PC.

Donata, on the other hand, couldn't look away.

"She's got a webcam," Donata replied softly, knowing Mick had a sixteen-year-old daughter who wanted nothing to do with him after being raised by her mother abroad. The sight of this girl on the screen had to suck all the more for him.

And yeah, it was tough for Donata to look at the footage, too.

But unlike Mick, Donata had just found a new mission in life because she recognized the young woman on the screen. Not the girl's name or any part of her identity, maybe, but Donata recognized the desperation. The determination to take charge of life even though you had so few options at that age.

Donata remembered the overwhelming desire to please a lover after being raised with little love to speak of. She understood the innocent willingness to do anything for a guy who showed you a few scraps of affection.

And worse, she knew what it felt like to be betrayed by that same person you once worshipped.

Because the girl on the screen had been Donata once. And not for all the world would Donata let this anonymous young woman face the private hell that she had.

SEAN BERINGER didn't like being in a police station on a good day. But pacing the corridors of the 10th precinct when he knew damn well the cops inside the media room were about to invade his private investigation of a so-called reality adult filmmaker had his blood simmering, his skin crawling and his head about ten minutes from exploding.

"Who's on this case anyway?" he asked a passing detective who'd grudgingly admitted the pending investigation since they used to walk a Harlem beat together back in the day.

Back when Sean was still naive enough to believe wearing a badge could actually accomplish something.

"Look, man, don't bust my balls about this. I only told you we were on the case because I thought you'd be satisfied someone was working it." The detective, ballistics expert Warren Vitalis, looked as though he wanted to say more as he rapped his pencil against a stack of papers at the desk sergeant's cubicle.

Sensing possible information, Sean forced himself to quit pacing and focus. He *had* made good friends on the force for nearly ten years. But he'd walked away from the NYPD after his sister was molested. Family trumped friends every time.

"Please say it's somebody good on this case and not some tight-ass yes-man." At thirty-two years old, Sean had battled a tendency to speak his thoughts most of his life, but he didn't even try to curb his mouth for the sake of a cop he'd probably walked a thousand miles with during their year of shared foot patrol.

"More of a yes-woman," Warren noted before pointing his pencil toward the media room as the door finally opened. "And I'm making no comment on the ass."

Sean followed his gesture toward the woman emerging with a determined strut, her curves cloaked under a conservative suit jacket and knee-length skirt but still obvious to any discerning male eye. Her hair was darker blond than the last time Sean had seen her—more natural-looking than the platinum Marilyn Monroe locks she'd once sported—but she still outlined her lips with bold red lipstick in a flagrant in-your-face to the stereotypes about women cops. Her audacious figure and heart-shaped face made her look more like an old-time gangster moll than a detective, but then, Sean had the benefit of seeing her at home in her old life before the decision to switch sides.

"No need for comment," Sean finally managed to say when he found his voice. Donata Casale was the very last person he'd expected to see walk out of that media room, although a few years ago he remembered hearing that she'd been trying to see what life looked like on the other side of the law. "An ass like that speaks for itself."

Warren smothered a laugh, but not soon enough to stop Donata from looking his way. Sean's way.

"Damn you, Vitalis." Straightening, Sean ignored the sexual zing a woman like Donata brought to any room. "The one time I manage to keep my commentary to a whisper you sell me out anyway."

The station quieted for a moment as petite Donata changed direction and came straight toward him. Sean was intrigued to note the way the whole precinct paid attention to her, and not necessarily in a good way.

You could tell the women who hadn't acclimated to the predominantly male world of a police station. They either ignored the men around them in a continual effort to distinguish themselves with kick-ass work and be accepted, or they tweaked the male egos around them at every turn in an effort to show their lack of concern for male approval.

Sean didn't have to ask which type of woman detective Donata Casale made. Her lipstick told the tale at ten paces.

"A P.I. in our midst?" Donata observed lightly, tugging her white shirt cuffs down as she approached. "Perhaps Mr. Beringer finds himself in need of professional assistance."

It had been four years since he'd faced off with

this woman, but from the glint in her eyes, Sean guessed she hadn't forgiven him for their last encounter. He also noted that the blouse under her conservative jacket appeared to be pure silk—a glitzy holdover from her old life, perhaps.

"Actually, I came here to *offer* assistance." He looked over her shoulder, hoping for an ally who didn't already hate his guts. "Is your partner around? I wouldn't want to get slapped with sexual harassment charges because we shared the same air space."

Apparently he hadn't completely forgiven *her* either. He hadn't realized he held a grudge until the pissy accusation left his lips. Then again he wasn't some navel-gazing sensitive guy to sit around and weigh his state of mind when there was work to do.

If his words found any leverage in this woman's conscience, she didn't show it. If anything, her deceptively innocent baby blues only narrowed in preparation for battle.

"Still finding it tough to keep your hands to yourself?" Her tight smile let him know that she'd entered this skirmish for show and not because she had any interest in a discussion with him. "It must be hell to discover you're so victimized by your libido, but I'll let my partner know about your offer."

Pivoting on her heel, she presented him with her back and walked away.

Definitely a tight ass.

And damn, but he'd let that conversation go to hell in a hurry.

Sean cursed himself for being a prick when he could have used a bit of goodwill from the investigating officer on this one. He definitely needed to work on the amount of free rein he gave his mouth, but not once in his life had he ever given his hands too much freedom when it came to a woman. Especially not a woman he held in custody, the way he'd once held Donata.

Swallowing his pride and praying for a little more reserve, Sean stalked after her, not giving a crap about the field day the rumor mill would surely have with this incident. He needed Donata's assurance she was going to back off this case and he wasn't leaving the building without it. Ignoring the whistles and the comments pelted his way as he dodged metal desks and dilapidated rolling chairs spilling into the aisles, Sean told himself he needed to mentally regroup.

Donata wasn't the same woman she'd been four years ago, and even then he hadn't understood her. He'd made a costly error in judgment with an old case when she'd been working in conjunction with the feds, but that was the price of taking risks in police work. You might make more headway in some cases, but following hunches could sometimes give you just enough rope to hang yourself.

Cornering Donata in the vacant break room, he helped himself to a powdered doughnut while she poured herself a cup of coffee nearby. He had no idea how to get back in her good graces, but this case was important enough that he'd try.

Clearing his throat, he lowered his voice and came straight to the point.

"I take it you're still pissed off about that night I arrested you?"

2

DONATA TOLD HERSELF that this man probably had no idea how badly his timing sucked.

In fact, she told herself *repeatedly* while she contemplated the added calories of coffee creamer and decided she'd rather not do the extra sit-ups required and she'd *really* rather not have this discussion with a man who'd caused her so much grief.

"You give yourself a lot of credit, don't you?" She turned to face him, clutching her coffee cup and hoping her nosier colleagues could restrain themselves from wandering in for at least a few minutes. No doubt the whole place would be buzzing about her run-in with the man whose accusations had been her biggest obstacle to overcome in securing a spot on the force.

Damn him for showing up today when she should be formulating a plan to unearth a first-degree pervert who was filming girls in their home bedrooms and then mass-marketing their mistakes for public consumption.

"Honestly, no. I only asked because the incident

seems like it's not going away until we deal with it, and I've really got to talk to you about your new investigation."

His sudden switch to seeming forthrightness caught her off guard even though that was exactly the same way he'd snuck under her radar long ago. She hadn't known what to make of a direct man back then and she sure as hell didn't know what to make of him now.

Everything about Sean Beringer was entirely too good-looking. He was the kind of man Donata had always avoided because she suspected a man like him would require far too much work. A woman who succumbed to an exterior that attractive would certainly spend half her time beating off other women with a stick. And—from a purely practical standpoint—a man like him would have to devote too much time to battling temptation continually waved under his nose.

He was tall, loose-limbed, broad shouldered. A hot body currently clothed in jeans, a Mets T-shirt and a long wool coat that a more discerning dresser would have paired with a suit. But the incongruity of the dress coat and the T-shirt did nothing to detract from the dark male beauty of deep-set hazel eyes under angular brows.

"What would you know about my caseload?" She sipped the coffee and wondered where Mick had gone. Shouldn't her partner be in on this conversation? He probably even knew Sean since they'd no doubt crossed paths when they were both detectives.

"I've still got a crony or two I can call on when I'm keeping tabs on a particular case." He leaned back against an ancient soda machine and watched her through his heavy-lidded eyes.

Had the ballistics guy—Vitalis, she seemed to remember—given Sean insider information? She'd seen them talking earlier when she first spied Sean, but she didn't want to believe the firearms analyst would do anything remotely shady. He struck her as an upstanding guy despite his intimidating looks.

"And just what are you keeping tabs on lately?" She knew he'd had a special interest in her former boyfriend, a mobster type she'd eventually sold out when she learned what kind of person he was beneath the expensive veneer.

It had taken her a long time to see herself as more than a naive female who'd fallen for a Svengali-style lover in an effort to get away from a crappy upbringing. But she *was* more than that. Her record on the force proved it and no innuendo from Sean Beringer could make her think otherwise.

"An adult filmmaking outfit that packages their illegal webcam footage as reality porn. I heard an arrest was made out on Long Island last week after a girl was molested by a guy who contacted her on the Internet."

Instantly alert, Donata was more than willing to put aside a good grudge against Beringer—temporarily at least—for the sake of her case. On a trip into Manhattan, Sara Chapman had indeed been molested by an older man she thought was a high school guy after a few online chats. Patrol officers had captured the perp without much trouble, but apparently further questioning revealed her molester had found her through her picture on a Web site advertising a reality porn DVD.

Her parents were devastated. Sara wasn't talking.

"Are you working for the family of the girl?" She knew rich people sometimes hired outside P.I. help if they were concerned the police couldn't get the job done.

"I've got a more personal interest. I've been following this case since you and I crossed paths four years ago."

She waited for him to continue, but he just turned and snatched another doughnut instead, wolfing half of it down and showering the break room floor with powdered sugar.

"Obviously there's more to this story if you're still pursuing leads on a case this old. Why don't I grab my partner and we can—"

"No." Sean imprisoned her arm before she could turn away to find Mick. "Don't you think we ought to work out the issues that are ours alone first before we go involving anyone else?"

His touch communicated to her more quickly than his words, the heat of his hand penetrating her jacket and warming her skin beneath. How long had it been since a man had touched her?

"Actually, no." She pulled out of his grip and set her coffee aside to devote her full attention to the conversation. "Private discussions were how we ended up in trouble last time, remember?"

Her heart pounded strangely, making her hyperaware of her body and the heat simmering inside it.

"No problems with remembering here." He held up his hands like a suspect trying to remind her he didn't have a weapon.

Except that he did. Sean Beringer possessed a boatload of sexual attraction that Donata didn't want any part of.

"Then why don't you let me get Mick and we'll make sure there are no more…incidents."

It was tough to think with him standing so close to her and suddenly she wanted to flee as far and fast as she could. A stupid reaction since she was on a four-year quest to prove to herself she was a woman of strength and integrity. But nothing made her feel weak as quickly as attraction to a man.

"Did you really think I was sexually harassing you back then?" Sean's forehead furrowed enough to let her know the idea bothered him.

"I—" She hesitated, not sure how to explain. "I thought you were hitting on me."

Her pulse fluttered in her throat at the memory of being in an interrogation room with him. She'd been working as an informant for the FBI, a position that left her in uncomfortable limbo selling out the ex-boyfriend she'd grown to despise but still needed to stay with. She'd looked like a guilty mobster's girlfriend to the outside world but inside she knew she was just a blind, stupid idiot who fell for a much older man with a worldly edge that appealed to dopey girls with no judgment.

"For the record, I would never hit on anyone in my custody when I was a cop, and I wouldn't think of it now that I'm a P.I." He backed away from her slowly, his dark eyes steady on her face. "I know I messed up your investigation with the arrest and I take full blame for not doing my homework where you were concerned. But I guarantee I'd never make a move on someone I arrested."

Gulping down more coffee to clear her head of wayward thoughts, Donata wondered if Sean ever hit on lady cops he worked with. A wholly inappropriate notion. She seriously needed to think about finding a lover to take the sexual edge off for her before she combusted from four years' worth of pent-up frustrations.

"Donata." A male voice called to her from the door and she looked up to see Mick holding his car keys.

"You're leaving?" She swallowed the urge to drag him into the break room by his collar. She needed the barrier of his presence to make sure her thoughts didn't linger on Sean as that potential lover.

"The school called. Katie's not in class today even though I dropped her off at school at seven-thirty." His square jaw tightened. "She's probably just playing hooky at a friend's house, but she's not answering her phone."

"Do you need help?" Concern for Mick's daughter had her halfway across the room.

"No. Just cover for me here." He nodded tersely at Sean. A nod of recognition. "I'll head out to Massapequa after I locate Katie and see what I can learn from the parents of the Chapman girl. I have the feeling the Long Island police will try to move jurisdiction there, but we're fighting to keep this case since she was molested in our jurisdiction."

Which meant she'd get stuck here with Sean. Alone.

"Call me when you find out anything." She could manage without Mick, couldn't she? She certainly owed him the time to take care of his family when he'd always been so good to her.

His support on the force had bought her far more credibility than her arrest record as a beat cop.

"Will do." He was gone two seconds later, leaving her in a precinct crowded with officers who resented her presence on the force and a P.I. who had every reason in the world to want to see her fail.

Donata against the world.

Wouldn't be the first time.

She spun on her heel to face Sean and caught him staring at her from his new perch on the break room table. Right beside the doughnuts. He'd obviously served his time on the police force given his love of the profession's notorious indulgence.

"Alone at last." He smiled crookedly at her as he tossed a balled-up napkin in the trash can and slid off the table to stand. "You think we can head somewhere more private now to clear up a few things? Seems like we both have reasons to want to keep this quiet."

"We can leave the precinct, but I don't have much time." Life experience had taught her not to linger with men who made her uncomfortable and she had no intention of ignoring that hard-won wisdom now when Sean's proximity made her skin heat and her throat go dry.

SEAN SENSED THE runaround when Donata tried to claim she suddenly needed to interview a witness on the NYU campus that afternoon. He tagged along for the ride, figuring she needed to settle down after the sudden way he'd reappeared.

But he drew the line at stepping into the role of her partner while she ran around New York pretending she didn't feel the sizzle that had damn well always been there between them.

Harassment my ass.

Maybe ice queen Donata had no clue what attraction felt like so she'd rather label it unwanted attention and shove it away from her with both hands than own up to her feelings. Whatever her reasons, he wasn't letting her stall tactics trip him up.

"I'm not going with you to interview any suspect that isn't directly related to the filmmaker case." He nodded toward a park bench in Washington Square, where students congregated between classes despite the recent bout of unseasonably cold October weather.

"Have a seat and we can exchange information so I can let you go about your day in peace, okay?"

She hesitated when her cell phone rang and she took the call with brusque efficiency before hitting the off button.

"Sorry about that, but I've got a lot on my plate today." She cinched the belt on her dark wool coat tighter. "Maybe we should reschedule this so we have more time?"

"So we have to wade through the awkwardness of seeing each other all over again?" He resisted the urge to pull her to the damn bench and sit her down because he remembered how much any extraneous touching set her off.

But damn. She was a tough case.

"You're right," she relented finally, walking toward the vacant bench under her own steam, her soft breath making a visible puff in the cold air. "I'd appreciate any information you can give me on the illegal filmmaker. I look forward to sending that particular creep to prison for a very long time."

"I don't think the actual producer is illegal." Sean didn't have any intention of sharing everything with her since he had worked his tail off to hunt down the bastard for himself.

"Of course he's illegal if he's filming underage girls." She filched two napkins from a coffee kiosk nearby and swiped them across the bench before taking a seat.

"What I mean to say is that he probably dabbles

on both sides of the business—legitimate and illegal—so that he's covering his butt with one for the other." He couldn't disguise the bitterness in his voice.

"You think he's distributing porn through traditional film venues?" She kept her voice low in deference to the hundreds of people who passed through the square even though no one paid them any attention. They were more alone here among hundreds than they had been in a precinct break room.

"No. I think he distributes the illegal stuff mainly online, but he cloaks his operations behind the front of a legitimate filmmaker." He knew all of it to be fact, actually, but he didn't want to reveal how deeply he'd immersed himself in this investigation just yet. And for all his efforts, he still didn't have a name to go with the profile.

"So how did you get involved with this shining example of humanity?" She tucked her hands into her coat pockets and stared out over the crowd gathering around two guys in red superhero capes who were playing guitars in exchange for donations.

"I left the force because my kid sister was molested by some guy she met on the Internet and the cops wouldn't do jack shit to nail the bastard." He dug a couple of bucks out of his wallet for the street musicians, appreciating the way the folk songs provided some mental distance from what he was saying.

Donata remained silent. Listening. Waiting.

"The guy who met her online found out who she

was after a video of my sister had been distributed without her knowledge. When she was eighteen, she had a webcam set up to send video of herself to her boyfriend but apparently the dude forwarded pictures to some trash sites with her personal information attached. That's how this other guy found her."

"Is she okay now?" Donata's hand landed gently on his arm, the unexpected touch more comfort than he would have expected from someone as seemingly reserved as her.

"She's put it behind her pretty successfully. In fact she lives ten states away and it pisses her off that I'm still on a quest to bring down the whole operation since it brings back bad memories. But I can't stand the idea of kids unknowingly exposing themselves to scumbags who will turn around and sell video snippets for a profit."

"And you've been after this group for how long?"

"I'd just started the investigation when I arrested you, so I guess it's been four years. But I'm on the verge of cracking the power behind the ring now…as long as the cops don't elbow their way in and mess up the sting I've got in the works."

Okay, that was a stretch. But he had names and addresses for hundreds of people who subscribed to the sites specializing in youthful exhibitionists, and that in itself made for powerful information.

"Basically, it's fourth quarter and you're asking me to take a knee while the clock runs out." Her hand slid away from his arm and back into her pocket. The crowd around the guitar players burst into applause at the end of the song.

"Is that a problem when you're already ahead in the game and victory is imminent?" He suspected from her suddenly rigid spine that she wasn't liking the idea.

"You forget we're playing for different teams. I don't have the luxury of working for myself and making my own calls on handling cases. I'm responsible to my department. To taxpayers."

Frustration pounded in his head as he began to see the many ways his operation could blow up in his face if the cops started crawling all over things.

"You don't understand how close I am to smoking out these bastards." No reasonable person would deny him this opportunity after all the years he'd put into cultivating inside contacts. "I've got a girl ready to sell out the filmmakers and put the last nail in the coffin for me."

If she didn't change her mind. Sometimes it was tough to tell with connections you'd made online.

"Sean, I appreciate that this case is personal for you, but you can't ask me to just pretend it doesn't exist when it comes under my jurisdiction. Half my precinct thinks I'm crooked anyway for reasons I'm sure you can appreciate."

He knew it had to be tough to cross over into the police world after she'd seen prison bars—if only briefly—from the inside. Still, it said a lot for Donata's character that she'd managed to wrangle her way into the NYPD at all.

Rising to his feet, Sean tossed the money in the open guitar box at the players' feet and turned back to her.

"All the more reason to steer clear of this investigation, Donata. The brains and the wallet behind the operation might belong to someone you know well." He dealt his best card to send her off the case for good. "My sources show your old pal Sergio Alteri is running his business as usual from a prison cell."

3

LATER THAT NIGHT, Donata didn't remember the details of how she'd got through the rest of the day.

Hearing her former lover's name cast into conversation like a gauntlet had scrambled her thoughts, feelings and kick-ass veneer until she'd had no choice but to make lame excuses to get away from Sean long enough to regroup. Reassess. And find out for herself how the hell her old boyfriend—the man who'd been the center of her world when she was a teenager, the man who saved her from an emotional breakdown when her father died—could have possibly orchestrated crimes from behind bars.

At home in her apartment on the Upper East Side, Donata stroked her tabby cat's head and clicked through her personal files on Sergio. Her first instinct had been to ignore Sean's suggestion that her ex could continue to exert power from a federal prison. But how naive would that be, especially when she'd seen organized crime up close and personal during her years with Alteri?

The buzzing of her apartment's intercom system

had her cat jumping off her lap a moment later and Donata rose to see who would be downstairs at 8:00 p.m. Neighbors knew better than to buzz her when they locked themselves out since she was super cautious about security.

"Yes?" Her building was an old brownstone between York and East End Avenue. Normally she appreciated the privacy of her homey little building with no doorman, but on nights like this when she was already jumpy she wondered if she'd be better off somewhere else.

Somewhere that Sergio would never find her if he decided to take revenge for all she'd done.

"Donata, it's me. Sean."

Relief washed over her for a moment before her heart stuttered and she found herself smoothing her fingers over her clothes, flattening wrinkles and assessing her appeal at this hour when her work clothes were in the hamper. Not that her appearance should matter, damn it.

But the idea of having him here, at her apartment, unsettled her. She liked to face professional acquaintances when properly armed in her I-mean-business suits, whereas at home she liked to remind herself of the femininity she stomped down all day.

"Can we talk about your investigation tomorrow?" Not having the man-woman skills needed to dance around this kind of sexual tension, Donata figured avoidance would be a good policy until she had Mick around as a buffer.

She'd used up all her steely reserve at work today. At home she took comfort in falling into more relaxed—less contentious—surroundings. She found herself wishing she had her cat to snuggle, but Duchess was hiding under a chair.

"No. You told me earlier today that we could talk later, remember?" Impatience laced his voice. "Would you just open the door so I can at least come inside? It's freezing out here."

Seeing no graceful way around it, she hit the button to admit him downstairs and prayed hard for a clear mind to at least muddle her way through a conversation. Mick had called her earlier, sounding as weary as she felt, to let her know his daughter had been at a friend's house but that he had some issues he needed to square away with Katie and was taking a personal day tomorrow. Not a problem for Donata, but it left her to contend with Sean—and the pressure to drop the case—on her own.

Something she damn well refused to be afraid of.

Still, it rattled her to realize she was raking her fingers through her hair while she waited for him to arrive at her third-floor apartment. In defiance of her stupid female primping, she purposely scrubbed her locks into disarray again. What did she care what she looked like to talk to a pit bull P.I.?

By the time the knock arrived on her door and she peered through the peephole, Donata's nerves were already stretched taut. Yanking open the door, she couldn't help but resent that he'd blasted right through the boundaries she worked hard to keep in place at the police station.

"I'm off duty, Beringer." She heard the bitchy tone in her voice but was powerless to call back the words.

"Didn't anyone warn you there's no such thing as off duty when you're a New York cop?" He seemed oblivious to her bad mood or else he was very good at ignoring people's boundaries. "And call me Sean. I think we've been through enough together to warrant a first-name basis, don't you?"

Ignoring the reminder of a most unpleasant evening spent in jail, she took a deep breath while she closed the door and bolted the lock, hoping to steady herself and instead inhaling the vaguest hint of aftershave.

She'd forgotten what it was like to be inside a man's personal space. She'd hardened her heart to Sergio long before she'd sold him out. Her need to punish him for breaking the law and his promise of faithfulness to her had helped her ignore the old tug of attraction she'd once felt. But she hadn't learned how to defuse the heat between her and the man now in her apartment. It would singe her if she wasn't careful.

"Fine, *Sean*. I knew what I was signing up for to be on the force." She backed away from him, retreating deeper into the safe haven of her home. "I'm just not used to tripping over pushy P.I.s at every turn on an investigation."

"Good cops cultivate their sources, they don't

lock them out." He followed her into the living area that doubled as her bedroom in the small space. "Nice place you've got here."

So technically, she had a man in her bedroom after a long, long time. A shiver accompanied the thought as her gaze lingered on the foldout sofa where she slept.

"Not quite as grand as my Long Island digs, but at least it's all paid for honestly." She'd inherited a house in the Hamptons from her father when she was eighteen and she'd used the proceeds from the sale to set herself up in this apartment with a nice savings account for a rainy day. Everything that Sergio had ever given her she'd donated to charity after the split.

She hated what it said about her that she'd been involved with a crook. The police background check may have forgiven the transgression, but forgiving herself was far more difficult.

"I knew four years ago that you weren't guilty of anything but poor judgment, Donata. I only made the big show of putting you under arrest in the hope you might spill something about Sergio's connections in the filmmaking industry." He took off his coat and tossed it on her couch, making himself at home before she'd invited him to stay.

The intimacy of the act suggested an ease around her that men didn't usually feel with a woman accustomed to being labeled "cold." One of the police cadets she'd gone through training with had gone so far as to suggest she could wither a man's sexual interest at twenty paces with just one glare. Not exactly flattering, but a helpful kind of superpower for a female who was scared spitless of dominating men.

And yet Sean remained immune to the glare.

"I knew you didn't have any evidence," she admitted, figuring she might as well come clean if they were going to work together. "And I could have called in my FBI connections to set things straight, but I figured the threat of me being busted would buy me street cred with Sergio. He was starting to get suspicious of me. The big bust happened just a few weeks later."

"So all that surly silent treatment was an act?" He strolled around her living room, checking the titles of the books on her shelves, the DVDs next to the TV and the wine bottles on the rack near the kitchen.

The attention to his surroundings was typical of a good cop and she wondered why he'd felt the police department couldn't bring his sister's molester to justice. The department always needed good investigators and she had the feeling his leaving was a loss for the city.

"I honestly didn't know of any connection Sergio might have had to the film industry. But as for the tough-girl behavior, I did a lot of acting those last few months with him." What scared her more were the hours where she'd forgotten it was an act, the dates they went on that had seemed like old times and had made her forget for a little while that she was staying with him only to bust him.

It had all felt so unclean. So dishonest.

"What about the harassment charges?" Sean turned on his heel to stalk straight toward her now, all pretense of interest in her apartment gone as he focused on *her.* "Was that an act to buy points with your boyfriend, too?"

"No." She stifled the impulse to step backward, away from him. "But I realized afterward that I was just scared and…acting out…to even the odds between us. For what it's worth, I'm sorry about that."

She'd rescinded her verbal accusation and refused to formalize it in writing after her head had cleared from the sensual haze that enveloped the room when she and Sean had been together.

"Luckily, I was already making plans to leave the department by then so it wasn't as big of a deal as it might have been." He stopped a foot from her, his sleekly muscular body making its presence felt even though he didn't touch her.

Four years ago she'd thought the resulting shaky feeling inside had been from harassment. Now she recognized it for what it had been all along.

She had the hots for Sean Beringer.

EVEN AS SEAN BEGAN to realize it had been a mistake to seek out Donata after hours, he still couldn't make himself back away from her.

He'd seen hints of the old over-the-top sexiness at the precinct today in the pure silk blouse she'd worn beneath her navy suit. The fire-engine-red lips had been another clue, even if the rest of her face hadn't been made-up.

But in the safety of her own apartment, she obviously gave her diva leanings more room to play. Her blue-and-yellow lace camisole blouse outlined spectacular cleavage while a fuzzy blue sweater was tied closed with a satin ribbon around her waist. The crocheted sweater was full of so many holes a man could see everything through it, from the spaghetti straps of the blouse to the hummingbird tattoo on her lower back that showed between her low-rise jeans and the camisole.

What man could see a tattoo like that and not fantasize about tasting it?

Exotic perfume clung to her clothes and her skin, a scent that hadn't been present during her workday. Most women came home and stripped away the material trappings of beauty but apparently Donata cloaked herself in sexy feminine decor the minute she left the police department behind. The thought of her switching roles like that turned him on at a primal level.

"What did you want to discuss?" Her throaty words floated through his consciousness to distract him when all he really wanted to do was close the space between them and see if she felt as good as she looked.

From the satiny blouse and the fuzzy sweater to the sleek silken swish of her hair, everything about Donata was a tactile temptation, begging to be touched.

Unfortunately, he wasn't in any position to cop a feel.

"I need to know where you're going with this investigation since our conversation ended prematurely today. You seemed freaked out about Alteri's possible involvement in the filmmaking scheme, and I'm here to ask you nicely to back off if you think you can't separate feelings for your ex from the job."

"How dare you insinuate I can't keep my personal feelings out of my work?" She lowered her voice to a fierce whisper even though there was no one around to overhear them. "It's because of me that Alteri is behind bars in the first place."

"Hey, I couldn't keep my personal life out of my work, which was why I left the force." Frustration replaced some of the heat between them and he was grateful for the impetus to back away. He didn't need attraction to Donata screwing him over now that he was close to finally busting the sleazy video outfit. He needed to know more about the Sara Chapman case to see if her situation coincided with some of the other girls' experiences of having their video images posted online.

Donata seemed to think over what he said, her arms folded tight while she stared up at a framed photo of herself as a flamboyantly dressed teenager with her arm wrapped around a skinny old guy wearing a Doors T-shirt and a poorly fitting dinner jacket.

Had she started dating ancient men that young?

Alteri had to have been twenty years her senior and this guy looked closer to thirty.

"I respect your need to go after somebody who hurt your sister." Slowly, Donata turned on him, her eyes wearier and wiser than he remembered. "In turn, you have to respect that I'm going to be all over this investigation. Not just because it's my job, but because I have a particular axe to grind with men who try to take advantage of innocents. That doesn't make me sloppy. That makes me driven."

He barely recognized the woman who delivered the words. Outside, she looked the same with her too-sexy clothes and killer body. But the steely strength that emanated from within—that was all new since the last time they'd crossed paths. This Donata was a woman with a mission and Sean thought any guy would be damn lucky to have her on his side.

Except he didn't want a professional partner. If she wanted to partner in other ways, however...

"Heard and understood. I appreciate the honesty when we—"

"You ready for some more?"

"What?" He blinked.

"Honesty." Cool purpose gleamed in her eyes and Sean got a mental picture of her heading up a board-room instead of a police investigation.

That mental picture lasted about three seconds before being replaced by one of Donata naked and in his bed, his fingers exploring the soft terrain beneath the hummingbird tattoo.

"Su-sure." He loosened his collar before he remembered he wasn't wearing a tie. Damned if a Mets batting jersey could strangle a man, but somehow, his managed to do exactly that.

"Focus on this case is important to me and I'm having a hard time finding it with you and me working on it."

Of all the things he might have expected her to say, this would have been the farthest from his mind. She couldn't honestly be…flirting with him?

"Are you coming on to me?" He'd gotten rusty at interpreting signals from women in the years since his wife had left him, so chances were good he'd read Donata wrong. But since he'd never had enough finesse to muddle through blindly when asking a direct question could clear up everything in an instant, he figured he had nothing to lose by confronting her.

"Just the opposite." She fidgeted with the long blue ribbon dangling from the bow where her sweater was tied closed. "I'm asking for your help in keeping our interaction as impersonal as possible given our…unusual history."

The way she said it made him wonder how much of those hours they'd spent together she remembered. When she had refused to call a lawyer and he had been hell-bent on interrogating her anyway. There had been anger, resentment and undeniable sparks.

"No one at that precinct gives a crap about the past. Cops are only interested in your present and future and what you're bringing to the table that will help catch crooks."

"Perhaps I'm less concerned with what my colleagues think than what I think." She released the ribbon and the satin fabric swung like a delicate pendulum for a moment before coming to rest on the snap of her jeans.

The sight of that sleek fabric pointing the way south on Donata's voluptuous body would have distracted him under the best of circumstances, but now when he was trying to navigate his way through her cryptic words…his brain seemed to short-circuit.

"I'm not getting it." The scent of her—darkly sexy and warmed by the heat of her skin—drugged any remaining sense right out of him. "You're going to have to spell it out for me, Donata, because I'm not following you."

"Then let me make it clear as crystal." She swept aside the hem of her loose sweater to cock a hand on one denim-clad hip. "I'm not even sure I like you, Beringer, but there's something undeniably sexual in the air when we're in the same room and I want to avoid that at all costs."

Okay, this he could understand. Something sexual? Yes ma'am. This was finally making sense.

"You don't mean sexual in the negative sense, right?" He just needed to get this one last point straight because no way, no how, would any woman accuse him of something like harassment again.

Thinking hot thoughts wasn't a crime. Just so

long as he didn't act on anything without two thumbs up from the woman in question.

"No. I mean sexual in the distracting sense and I'll tell you right now I'm not going down that path with any man who knew me back in my questionable youth."

Her eyes were so cool and remote that he couldn't reconcile her overtly sexy exterior with the uptight words.

"I met you four short years ago. Hardly during your childhood." Reason clamored through the haze of lust in his brain, urging caution.

"But you saw me in the setting of the criminal underworld."

"You were working undercover."

"As an informant, not a paid detective. Big difference in respectability, don't you think?"

A knock sounded at her door before he could pick apart how ludicrous it was for her to write him off because they met under inauspicious circumstances. But then, he was too rocked by her admission that he distracted her to process anything else with much speed.

"Yes?" Donata answered the door after peering through the peephole.

A middle-aged woman wearing a long caftan waited on the threshold, a mug of something steamy in one hand and a FedEx package in the other.

"Sorry to interrupt." The woman peered over Donata's shoulder to take a visual inventory of Sean and for a moment she seemed to forget what she was saying.

Obviously, his charm still worked. Just not on the right woman.

"That's okay, Charlene. Did you need anything?" Donata's clipped tones were completely at odds with the sweet words she used to employ around her old boyfriend.

"Oh. Um, yes." The woman thrust a box through Donata's doorway. "One of your deliveries came to my door by mistake."

Thanking her, Donata took the package and closed the door even though the woman clearly had been angling for an invitation inside.

"Do you do this to every woman you meet?" Donata hissed out a breath between her teeth, somehow finding him at fault for her neighbor's nosiness.

"I'm sure she just wanted to know who you were hanging out with these days." Although, judging by Donata's quick squashing of any attraction between them, maybe there wouldn't be any hanging out involved.

"Yeah, tell me another one." She squinted at the box and frowned. "The shipping label doesn't look right."

He looked over her shoulder but didn't see anything unusual.

"There's no bar code. No return address." She spoke softly to herself as she reached for the pull-tab to open the package while Sean sought a way to get their conversation back on track.

He needed to leverage information from her on this case, convince her to let him proceed applying pressure in non-traditional venues because he couldn't allow the scumbags who'd hurt his sister to walk away.

"Oh God."

Donata dropped the manila envelope she'd pulled from the FedEx box.

"What?" Instantly on alert, Sean shifted his attention to her. He bent to retrieve the padded envelope and noticed her hands shook as he set it on her coffee table.

He wasn't rude enough to look inside the package, but he was curious enough to note the corner of one document stuck out the open end. It appeared to be a photograph or short stack of photos, the size of the corner suggesting they were large and glossy color prints.

"They're photos of me from when I was with Sergio." Her voice bore none of the steely determination he'd heard from her earlier. The hitch in her throat and high pitch quavered closer to tears. "The son of a bitch must have kept them for their future blackmail potential."

That didn't sound good. And judging by the suddenly chalky pallor of her skin, he'd say the photos weren't your garden-variety vacation shots.

"Are they…compromising?" He suddenly wondered if this case they were pursuing could possibly be even more personal to Donata than it was to him.

"If you mean are they naked, the answer is yes. Go ahead and have a look, Beringer, and you'll see just how bad of a girl I once was."

4

"WAS THERE A LETTER with it?" Using the corner of his T-shirt to prevent any extra fingerprints, Sean picked up the box the envelope had arrived in without looking at photos that obviously embarrassed her. "The package couldn't have gone through FedEx with no labels. Somebody must have dropped it in front of your neighbor's place."

"I didn't see a note." Donata shook her head, her pale skin even whiter than usual as she stared at the envelope full of photos. "I didn't even look at all the pictures."

And who could blame her? She had to have busted her tail to climb the ranks of the police force the way she did, even with key recommendations from two FBI agents she'd worked with to get the dirt on her old boyfriend. No wonder she wasn't in any hurry to look through a package of photos that could destroy her career or—at very least—shred her credibility.

"I'll look through them if you want me to, Donata. But if you'd rather keep them private, I'm going to ask you to scan through everything before we decide what to do next." He knew he wasn't the cop here, but she didn't look ready to take on the lead investigator role right now.

This had to suck big-time for her.

What the hell kind of partner did she have to leave her hanging on a huge case like this? He knew of Mick Juarez's reputation on the police force, but the guy sure didn't seem to be living up to it today. But Sean prayed she didn't want him to take a peek because he didn't know how well he'd handle seeing naked pictures of this woman. And she definitely didn't need a P.I. with a hard-on trying to straighten out this mess.

She nodded. Blinked.

"I'll do it." With shaking fingers, she reached into the envelope and withdrew the stack of photos, keeping the backs of the prints to him. About ten in all. "I don't see any— Wait."

Sean set the box by the front door as a reminder to her to bring it into the lab guys tomorrow so she could have it run for prints. The incident might not have anything to do with her investigation, but she'd want to follow up on it anyhow.

"You got something?"

"Yeah. It says, 'I have a few photos that will make nice wall art for the 10th precinct. Leave the filmmaker case alone and I'll keep the pictures our secret.' There's no signature."

The note made him wonder how explicit the photos might be but he didn't think he could handle that discussion right now with his thoughts running wild. His imagination was too damn vivid when it came to supplying possibilities.

"Your friends at the FBI would be interested in this. Even without being processed through FedEx, using their packaging might make a case that this was a federal crime." The selfish half of him didn't want the feds swarming around any more than he wanted city cops treading over his terrain.

But if Sergio had his people coming after Donata personally, Sean could see the benefit to creating a world of trouble for the prick.

"No." She slid the stack of photos into the envelope and laid the pack on her coffee table. "This is my case and I'm not handing it over to you, or the FBI or anyone else."

Resolve glittered in her blue eyes.

"I know this is a low blow—"

"It's more than that." She paced around the living room and pulled open the front of a wooden cabinet that turned into a minibar, her hand shaking ever so slightly. "This is his way of trying to tear down everything I've worked for. My self-respect. My standing in the workplace. My first real career."

Sean had an inkling how hard it must have been for her to come up through the ranks to get where she was today. Beyond the obvious physical challenges for a woman who was all of five foot four, Donata had to pass the interviews, the character background check that would have grilled her on her relationship with a criminal, and then there would have been the high chance of prejudice within the department. No matter how good her intentions as an informant, her fellow cops couldn't have appreciated her time spent living with a well-known gangster.

And naked pictures of her on the loose would cause more of an uproar given her history. Not to mention the problems it would cause for her in getting her job done. Her colleagues might have trouble taking her seriously and *damn it* but he didn't want anyone else seeing her naked.

"Let me handle this and we can keep it out of the police department. If I need backup, or I think you could be in physical danger, I can call in the FBI instead of the NYPD." He'd been working on this case for so long he'd accumulated thousands of names of subscribers to the illicit reality porn services. As soon as he had enough proof to arrest a few of the key figures, he'd take down supporters of the industry all over the country. Restricting NYPD's access to anything that touched the investigation was a win for him and a win for Donata's career.

She set a bottle of Amaretto on the bar with excessive force, inciting a clink of every glass hanging upside down over the minibar.

"Damn it, Sean, will you wake up and see that this isn't about what you want anymore?" She hadn't even poured her drink when she snapped the cabinet closed again and walked. "I understand that you're pissed off on your sister's behalf and I don't blame you. But there are more girls than her getting hurt every day that you wait to break this case."

"Jesus, Donata. It's never been about me." How could she think that when he'd thrown his whole life into turmoil by quitting the force so he could investigate this ring the way he wanted and not the slow way some giant bureaucratic agency wanted it handled? His choices had cost him plenty.

"Come on, Sean. You think I don't know why you've been waiting to blow the whistle on this operation?" She shook her head as she picked up a book of matches and lit a fat candle with four separate wicks. "I know enough about being an outsider to recognize someone else's need for vindication. But this can't be the story of ex-cop vigilantism that you want it to be. Too many people are getting hurt along the way."

"You couldn't be more wrong." At least, he wanted her to be wrong because he sure as hell didn't like the picture of him she painted. "I'm just trying to make sure there's enough evidence to put this crew away for a long time. You know as well as I do, they'll be back on the streets abusing kids in no time otherwise."

"Fine. We'll make sure we've got evidence. I'll go through the files tomorrow and I'd appreciate it if you'd share what you know so we can move forward. But I can guarantee you, I'm not walking away from this."

For the first time since he'd become reacquainted with Donata Casale, Sean realized he couldn't ask her to turn her back on the case.

A fact which left him working with a fiery dynamo of a woman to close an investigation that had become a huge powder keg.

There wasn't a chance in hell they'd come through this unscathed.

"NO FINGERPRINTS on the box," Mick reported after hanging up the phone with the lab two days later. "And since Sergio Alteri is in jail, he has an iron-tight alibi on this one. Any ideas where to go now?"

Donata spun in her desk chair, unable to think clearly about the case with Sean an ever-present fixture in her brain. Desks and detectives blurred as she twirled back and forth, searching for ideas and wondering if she'd ever make peace with her past.

She'd confided in Mick about the pictures since she trusted him to be discreet. He hadn't asked to see the photos, nor had he tried to strong-arm her into entering the pictures for evidence, for which she'd be eternally grateful. Mick was a good friend and damned attractive too. But the chemistry just wasn't there—not the way it had always been present for her whenever Sean walked in a room.

"The prison log shows a lot of letters going in and out of Ray Brook Correctional Facility, but no visitors for Alteri." That made the investigation tougher, but the news had pleased Donata on a personal level since she liked to think that his so-called friends had all forsaken him. Even his mistress—the obnoxious Rosie Gillespie—hadn't bothered to keep in touch.

"We'd better get a list of his correspondents. In the meantime, I'm meeting with Sean today to go over his evidence again since he's been working on connected cases for a while." She felt self-conscious bringing Sean up and couldn't say why, except that she'd been thinking about him far too often. He'd surprised her with his thoughtful handling of the picture episode the other night. "We didn't come up with any great ideas the first time, but I was still reeling from the appearance of the photos. I think today we're going to visit some of the more prominent webcam streams and see what happens when we subscribe to the services advertised online."

And wouldn't that be interesting to spend time in close quarters with a man who occupied a few too many of her fantasies the past few days?

"You're traveling risky terrain." Mick didn't approve of methods that involved her in anything illegal.

Three days ago she would have nixed the tactic, too. But that was before the stakes had been upped. Clearly, whoever had been planting webcams in teenagers' bedrooms was starting to sweat the possibility of getting caught.

"I'll be careful." She wouldn't jeopardize her career—or her shot at destroying an illegal business making a bundle off insecure girls.

"What if it's not Sergio behind it all, Donata?" Mick stirred his coffee slowly, the inevitable clank of his spoon a rhythmic ringing that seemed to echo his subtle warning.

"We'll get this guy either way."

"Just don't let your anger at him cloud your judgment."

Good advice. Except that she wondered if he thought her judgment might be off when it came to the case—or when it came to men in her life.

SEAN RAN HIS P.I. business out of a squat building in SoHo. He owned a storefront on the street and lived in the loft a few stories above it. The loft was Donata's destination now that it was after business hours even though they would be technically talking business.

She traced the neatly etched lettering on the glass door at street level that read Beringer Investigations. Sean's neighborhood had a warmer feel than her more sterile residential street full of working couples and upwardly mobile singles who left the neighborhood vacant during the day. Here, a nearby coffee shop kept a busy flow of foot traffic and the funky old architecture of the building across the street had attracted a photo shoot with two stylists scampering in and out of a fashion scene featuring an elegant-looking man and woman wearing long spring jackets while they battled playfully with closed umbrellas as if they were swords.

What was the world coming to when the only people having fun had been paid for their elaborately staged efforts?

Turning the doorknob, Donata tried to remember

the last time she'd felt as light-hearted as the people in the photo shoot pretended to be. Unfortunately, her most fun memories had all been tainted with the later realization that her partner in fun had been a liar and a cheat, and now possibly a perv to boot.

Inside the building, a second door labeled Beringer Investigations was closed while an old elevator sat side by side with a staircase. Donata started up the stairs as Sean's directions had suggested, and after a single flight she heard a door open above her then a familiar voice shouted down.

"You won't believe this."

She looked up to see Sean hanging over the rail two floors above. The central staircase wound around a corridor open throughout all the floors. Apparently he owned this side of the building, while a landlord rented apartments to a handful of tenants on the other side of the building that opened onto the next street.

She'd half hoped she'd imagined the sizzle factor between them, but it was back again in full force judging by the pleasant buzz of attraction humming through her veins just looking at him. So frigging inappropriate. But she liked the way he treated her with a certain amount of respect. Sean's attraction communicated itself through subtleties rather than a gaze fastened to her cleavage like some guys.

Too bad she'd screwed up so badly with him four years ago when he'd taken her in for questioning. No way would this guy ever act on the heat between them now. Not that she necessarily wanted him to. But she still regretted the misunderstandings of their past.

"What won't I believe? Did the bad guys confess?" She picked up her pace, her aerobic conditioning one of the sweetest side benefits of her job. She could bang out flights of stairs as easily as most people strolled through a park.

"No." He dangled some black cords over the stairwell. "After I set up that fake ID online I've got pervs from all over the country mailing me electronic equipment to help me set up a Web site with high-quality imagery."

She closed the distance between them, winding her way around the highest landing to see the gadgets he'd been showing her—and swallowing back some major drool over the man. A webcam was the only item she recognized in a small pile of technological-looking loot.

"How can anyone send you equipment without knowing your real name?" Her years as a patrol officer had given her face-to-face experience with more overt crime—rape and domestic abuse. Drug sales gone bad and drive-by shootings. The Internet criminal was new to her, although she'd read case files on a few online money-making rackets. Normally, the NYPD handed over those investigations to specialized departments.

"Some guy who's buying into the fact that I'm a teenaged girl showed me how to set up a wish list through an online superstore. Anyone who knows my wish list name can send a present through the site while my personal information remains anonymous."

"And you wished for a webcam?" She didn't want to break department protocol to make this bust, and she wondered how this tactic would go over in court.

"Of course not. I just went along with it to let the guy think I was a teenage girl. I put some bubblegum pop CDs on there and other stuff then forgot about it until a box showed up with all kinds of equipment that would allow me to set up a video feed so I can show myself to admiring fans."

"I think the jig is up because you'll never pass for a girl." She had to laugh at the image because if she thought for too long about the young women who got sucked into that kind of life in a bid for friendship or acceptance—or even money—Donata wouldn't be able to do her job.

"So we'll play shy and see how much effort these guys go to in order to push their victims into the spotlight. I'm starting to think there are a hell of a lot more people at work on these kinds of schemes than just the filmmaker who packages the video snippets for sale." He shoved the equipment into a shipping box and Donata saw that the pieces were labeled as a four-port hub that advertised it could be used for multiple cameras. Another box contained a memory upgrade.

Her insides felt hollow to glimpse this new world of potential violation for mixed-up teenagers. She knew how it felt to have compromising photos follow you through life. These kids wouldn't just have a few pictures to worry about. They'd have hours of video footage readily available online. How badly would that suck?

She followed Sean into his apartment. The expansive space was circled with windows on two sides thanks to its corner position. The real estate had to cost a small fortune.

"The P.I. business is paying you well." She wandered over to the closer wall of windows and looked down at the street. She'd waited until after her regular shift to work with Sean, so by now the commuter traffic was kicking into high gear. Cars had their lights on because, even though the sun hadn't set yet, twilight would be stealing through the sky soon. By the time the bridge and tunnel crowd arrived home, it would be fully dark.

"Not really."

"I'm sorry. That was a tacky observation by me, anyway." She rolled her eyes, wondering if she'd ever shed the lower-class sensibilities that had come with her upbringing. Sergio had always been too easily impressed by money, a quality she definitely didn't want to share.

She liked seeing this side of Sean. The private side. His home was tasteful but comfortable and it smelled vaguely of him. Was it possible to be turned on by an apartment? Her mood lightened a bit at the thought.

"Not at all. I'm sure the investigators who work

for big-time divorce attorneys with wealthy clients probably make a bundle, but that's not really my style." Sean set the box on a massive cherry desk that sat in one corner of the loft that looked like a home office. "I inherited this half of the building from an aunt. My sister used to live on the next floor down before she moved out west."

"It seems like a great neighborhood." She wondered how he got along with his sister and if she'd moved away to escape some of his staunch protection. But Donata didn't want to pry. Removing her coat, she stared at the computer screen where Sean seemed to be in the middle of a chat room discussion.

"It's usually fairly quiet around here." He took her coat and pulled out the sole desk chair for her. "Have a seat and you can see what I've been looking over this afternoon. Did Mick tell you he checked his daughter's computer history recently and he found a bunch of visits to a teen Web portal that's well known for attracting pedophiles in addition to the regular clientele?"

She took a seat beside him, heart jumping just a bit. She found herself enjoying the reality of being attracted to a man who wouldn't manhandle her, a man who'd made it a personal crusade to save unsuspecting women from the heartaches that awaited them in the form of online predators. Women could dish about men's butts or abs all day long, but at the end of the day, that dedication to a worthy cause seemed way more attractive than nice pecs.

Although, wouldn't you know, Sean happened to have both.

"When did you talk to Mick?" Call her paranoid, but something struck her as strange about a P.I. and a cop who'd been marginally suspicious of one another suddenly developing enough rapport to discuss an ongoing case.

Without her. And yes, she'd be the first to admit she carried a chip on her shoulder when it came to precinct politics.

"I called the station a few minutes before you arrived to see if you'd left yet. When Mick picked up your extension, he mentioned the concerns for Katie, who's been lying to both parents about her whereabouts lately."

Donata clicked through some of the windows Sean pointed out while they spoke, including the Web community Mick's daughter had been visiting. Some of the teens' sites were innocuous enough and others had a decidedly sexual tone although none of them came close to the content on the subscription sites Sean had bought into for the sake of the investigation.

They worked side by side for the first hour or so, with Sean bringing Donata up to speed on the investigation he'd been picking away at for years. His sister's molester had been locked up long ago, but that hadn't been justice enough for him and frankly, Donata could understand why. The bastard who'd hurt his sister had found her through the massive network of sex criminals linked by seemingly end-less online communities. And Sean wanted to bring down as many of those communities as possible. The ones who trafficked in webcam porn or more innocent webcam footage turned into porn by spurn-ed lovers or boyfriends as an act of revenge were the highest on his list.

Donata's eyes were starting to cross two hours later when she hit a site that advertised innocent girls showing off on their teen webcams. Most of the footage looked harmless enough—girls having pillow fights at sleepovers with an occasional hint of undies and other video clips that were probably posted by the unsuspecting girls themselves. She was about to leave the site when a name on the index caught her eye.

Donata.

Curious, she moved the mouse over the name. It wasn't that common, but she'd certainly come across it a few other times. Still, when you had a more unusual name, you felt a little sense of kinship with anyone who shared it. Or maybe that was just her. Her life wasn't exactly overflowing with friendships and supportive connections so maybe she tended to seek out whatever ties she could in a hostile world.

Sean's computer was fast, but the graphic images still moved slower than other pages and it took a moment for the photo to load. As soon as the top band filled the width of the screen, however, Donata knew she wasn't going to find any kinship here. She recognized the backdrop for the picture before the rest of the image came over the screen.

Sean had disappeared into the kitchen to grab them each a beer, but he returned now to settle their drinks on the folded sports section of the *Times*.

"I don't know why the bastard thought he could blackmail me into staying off the case when he'd already turned my photos into public property." She couldn't look away from the ancient picture of herself, the one she'd let her ex-lover take in a moment of trust. It would have been like looking away from an oncoming train wreck.

What did it matter if Sean saw the photo now that people all across the country had the option to copy and save it to their hard drives? Clearly, she wasn't going to be able to keep all her dirty little secrets as private as she would have liked. Her few moments of reckless stupidity had been captured in full color to haunt her for the rest of her days.

And the tug of her attraction to Sean—something normal and healthy, even if she never acted on it— would be tainted by the ugliness of her old life.

"Holy hell," Sean whispered, his voice deep and ragged a few inches from her ear as he leaned closer to the computer screen to get a better view. "That's you?"

5

SEAN DIDN'T WAIT for her answer.

He grabbed his beer off the desk so fast it spilled out the top of the long neck, trailing dark lager across the back of his hand as he made tracks away from the computer screen and away from the image now deep-fried into his mental sexual circuitry. He didn't know whether he needed the cold beer more for his dry mouth or to combat the raging hard-on he'd fought successfully sitting next to Donata for two hours until that damn photo materialized on his monitor. Drink the brew? Or pour liberally over his lap?

God. Damn.

He settled on a long drink, knowing neither option would solve his problem. He'd never forget the image of Donata strapped to a board that might have been a weight bench or an incline sit-up support. Thick black strips of leather wound around her naked body to hold her in place so that the juncture of her thighs was covered—barely—although her breasts were visible between two other strips. Her hair, longer then, spilled over the board in a mass of messy curls and her eyes were rimmed in black like a rock star or an Egyptian queen. A tattoo of a rose in full flower had been inked inside one hipbone and her spread legs seemed to strain against the bonds. But she'd been staring at the camera with an exaggerated pout on her red-painted lips as if to assure the viewer her light S&M pose was only for show.

And what a hell of a show it had been.

He looked through the bottom of his suddenly empty beer bottle and wondered where it had gone.

"Yeah, it's me." Donata's voice didn't penetrate his consciousness for a long moment after she spoke. "I guess we can't hide my past any longer, but I appreciate you not pushing me to make the photos part of police records when the hard copies arrived a few days ago. I'll add the information first thing tomorrow morning and—"

She broke off suddenly, snapping Sean out of his drooling stupor enough to see her bury her face in her hands. He'd been so caught up trying to extinguish the heat the image inspired he forgot all about how she might feel.

He'd never been accused of being Joe Sensitive, but even he had to admit his reaction had been purely a selfish one.

"I can get that picture taken down." He blurted the words, not quite remembering what she'd been saying but figuring any woman would want that kind of photo of herself out of circulation. "I know a guy who's great with that kind of thing. He can redirect the link to a Christian Web site or the NYPD FAQ on reporting a crime or something to send surfers running."

Sean would call the guy tonight, in fact, because the idea of anyone else looking at Donata that way pissed him off on a deep level. He couldn't help the irrational impulse that wanted *him* to be the only guy to see her naked.

And not just because some photo turned him on. If he was honest with himself, he'd have to admit he'd been seriously attracted to her long before now. Right from that first day they'd met and he'd put her under arrest.

Maybe that's why her accusation had stung so much. With another woman he might have blown off the words as the usual BS some women flung at a cop in an effort to be set free. But in Donata's case, he had been checking her out, even if he was damn sure he hadn't communicated as much with his hands or with his words.

"No." She pushed away from the computer, distancing herself from the photo she'd minimized at the bottom of the screen. "As much as I appreciate that offer on a personal level, I can't allow you to contaminate a case by tampering with potential evidence."

There were shadows under her eyes he hadn't noticed earlier and he wondered how much extra time she'd been spending on this investigation.

"What evidence?" He couldn't tamp down the surge of annoyance at the hypercautious approach police were too often forced to take in deference to an overworked justice system that would toss a case out for the most peripheral of reasons. "You're investigating an unsuspecting exploited teenager whose bedroom adventures are being mass-marketed for profit, not some dime-a-dozen Web site with titillating photos. Do you think for one minute your partner would hesitate to act if there were pictures of his daughter on this site?"

"She's a minor." Donata twisted a loose knob on his top desk drawer, spinning the old nickel hardware in circles since it refused to tighten properly anymore.

"So were you when these were taken." He didn't give a rat's ass how emphatic she was about her case. The picture was coming down tonight as soon as he made a phone call.

"Yes, but—" The chirp of her cell phone interrupted them, and she tugged the handset out of her purse. "Casale."

When her brow furrowed in concentration, Sean took the opportunity to give her some privacy and to make a call of his own in the bedroom. He'd have his techie friend copy down all the necessary server information and linking codes to Donata's picture in case the Web site could lead them anywhere, but Sean refused to wait for the official police department blessing to act. Donata's tenuous hold on credibility could be destroyed by then if he didn't do something.

He just hoped his friend could accomplish the job with his eyes closed, because Sean damn well wouldn't allow even one more person to see the sizzling woman beneath Detective Casale's clothes.

DONATA CLOSED HER PHONE after talking to Mick, knowing she ought to call it a night and go home but not sure where to find the energy. Seeing the photo of herself on the Net that anyone could access had shocked her at first, then drained her dry of any emotional connection to the picture.

Since Sean had disappeared into a back room, she maximized the photo at the bottom of his computer screen to stare at this ghost of her former self again. She studied the woman swathed in leather straps and looking entirely too sure of herself. From a purely objective standpoint, she looked damn good. Not air-brushed perfect, but strong and sexy even in a pose of exaggerated submission.

Running her finger over the line of her thigh on the screen, Donata remembered how much sexual play had gone into setting up the shot. She'd gently kicked Sergio away every time he came closer with another strap of leather, requiring him to kiss her and stroke her into playing along with his game. And she had played along. At the time, she'd felt very much in control of the situation, so certain of her love for her man and confident in his love for her.

That confidence and happiness radiated from the photo, which perhaps was what made it all the more difficult to look at now. The photo made her feel naive all over again, a sensation she despised. Even worse was the sense of shame that went along with it.

And yet…

She had no reason to feel guilty. She wasn't the first underage female to play with fire in the form of sex with an older man and she wouldn't be the last. Her grandmother had married a much older man and had spoken of her daughter's marriage to a high school friend with such scorn that Donata had opted to follow in her grandmother's footsteps. Of course, Granny hadn't gotten involved with a gangster, marrying a local plumber instead of hooking up with a man who never seemed to work but always had spending cash.

"Everything okay?" Sean returned, his bare feet so quiet on the hardwood floors that she hadn't heard him until he was close enough to see the computer screen.

Shame creeping back into her consciousness, she tamped it down, downsizing her feelings along with the image in a pitiful attempt at coping with the situation.

"Yes. Mick just wanted to let me know Mrs. Chapman called the station to suggest maybe it was her daughter's boyfriend who sold the webcam images of Sara." Her heartbeat tripped in awkward time as she looked up at Sean, the thoughts she'd been having about her sexual past somehow churning up carnal hungers. "Mick's going back out to Long Island tomorrow to question the boyfriend while I work the technological angle."

She sensed the heat in her face, felt the warmth pulsing under her skin and wished she'd slipped out of the apartment while Sean had been on the phone. She had no business thinking about him...*that* way.

Yet the more she told herself that, the more her brain seemed to force-feed her sexual suggestions. She saw disjointed images of herself undressing Sean, of them entwined together on the sofa that lay not five feet away, of Sean's hands wrapping lengths of leather around her too-hot body.

Abruptly, she stood.

"I'd better go." She leaned over the desk to retrieve her purse but he stopped her with a light touch to one shoulder.

"Wait." His hand barely grazed the fabric of her angora sweater, a fuzzy red V-neck she'd fallen in love with because of the decadent softness.

She hated knowing that he hesitated to touch her more than that because she'd threatened him with a sexual harassment suit eons ago, back in her former life when she'd been a certifiable idiot.

"I can't." She couldn't be around him when she felt so keyed up, so keenly aware that she'd lost her sexual self when Sergio betrayed her with a tart named Rosie and with his greed for money.

Donata had lost more than her sexual confidence though, since she'd ultimately realized what attracted her to Serg—his confidence, his ability to protect her—had later been the very traits to bite her in the butt. He'd been domineering and possessive with her while keeping his own options wide open. Was it any wonder she doubted her own judgment when it came to men now?

But then the light touch on her shoulder turned into a gentle stroke of her cheek and her knees nearly melted underneath her.

"Please." That one word held her in place, captive to whatever he might say.

She nodded. Waited. Tried not to breathe in his musky male scent for fear she'd end up returning the favor of his touch.

"You have no reason to be embarrassed about a picture taken in the heat of passion."

He thought that's why she was sprinting for the door? Embarrassment? While it might be easier to let him think so, she hated for him to believe her that weak.

"I'm not embarrassed." She refuted the accusation even before she'd come up with another excuse. "At least not anymore."

"No? Then why the hasty exit when we didn't even clarify where we're going from here?" His hand remained on her cheek, his thumb too close to her mouth. He stared at her for a long moment, his gaze dipping down to her lips and then back to her eyes. "You don't still have…feelings for this guy?"

"Are you kidding?" She hadn't expected him to

ever think that. "I'd rather have my kinky photo posted at the precinct than see my hoodlum ex again."

"Then what gives with the retreat?" His forehead furrowed with concern and it was all she could do not to close her eyes and lean into his touch.

But with all her energy focused on standing very, very still, Donata didn't have enough mental power left over to concoct a plausible explanation, leaving her no choice but to go with the truth.

"As much as I resent the man who took that photograph, the picture reminds me of all the sex I'm no longer having."

She'd been so intent on turning her life around and carving out a noble profession for herself that she kept her body, her heart and her feelings under lock and key. And although her heart seemed content to stay there, her body was making a hell of a case to be free.

Sean lowered his hand, removing his fingers from her cheek and leaving only the heat of the touch behind.

"You're thinking sex thoughts?" One eyebrow lifted in mild surprise.

"What? That's never happened to you before?" She knew she should back away, head for the door before she sacrificed any more pride, even though the conversation was taking an interesting turn.

She couldn't afford to let her guard down too much around this man.

"I'm not at liberty to say, given our history." The steely note in his voice reminded her of the way she'd panicked four years ago when he came close to her.

She hated that she'd started them off on bad footing, but she'd be damned if it would keep them from having a working relationship. And just now, she had an idea how she could level the playing field.

An unorthodox idea, maybe, but it would definitely keep Sean on his toes.

"Is that right?" She looked him in the eye, hoping she could carry off her plan. "Maybe this will help jar your memory and spur some thoughts of your own."

She wound her hand around the back of his neck to pull him closer, arching up on her bare toes to brush her mouth over his. Heat flared inside her at the slow, easy slide of her lips against his. Her breasts tightened against the silken fabric of her bra and she imagined how easy it would be to ease that ache if only she could lean into him, rub herself against the hard plane of his chest.

Vivid visions scrolled across her thoughts, making it nearly impossible to pull away even though she knew that's what had to happen. She'd be the worst kind of hypocrite if she fell into his arms tonight after raising the roof about his long, lingering looks once upon a time.

"There," she whispered, breaking off the kiss and managing to insert a half inch of space between them. "Now you can pay me back with a harassment threat of your own. Clearly, I was the aggressor this time. I promise I won't deny it in the morning."

Her heart skip-hopped as she breathed in his

scent, his nearness, his maleness. Her senses seemed heightened as she processed the sound of her breathing, the quiet hum of the electronics on the desk and the inevitable sounds of the city drifting up from the street below.

And then her hyperconcentration shattered as Sean slid his arms around her waist and kissed her. *Really* kissed her.

His was no gentle brush of mouths but a full-on assault. He slanted his lips over hers as if to improve the angle of access and his tongue flicked over the quivering softness of her lower lip. She closed her eyes in an effort to sink deeper into the moment, to give herself over to all that she'd been denying. She wanted this, wanted *him,* with a fervor she couldn't refuse.

Her lips parted under the expert sweep of his tongue, her whole body opening itself to whatever pleasures the night might offer. The time for rational thinking had fled, disappearing about the moment Sean had first touched her cheek. She couldn't pretend she didn't want to follow the heat that existed between them.

A low hum of approval emanated from her throat, the same sound a woman makes when tasting the first bite of warm chocolate cake. And yet this bliss was only a precursor of delights she knew awaited them if she dared push this further.

Heat pooled between her thighs at the thought and her hands gravitated to Sean's shoulders. She couldn't wait to get her hands on him—all over him—but she also needed the support of his strength when she was melting with long-suppressed desires. Her fingers dug into the cotton softness of his T-shirt to feel the warmth from his skin beneath.

So. Damn. Good.

Her breasts flattened against the plane of his chest, spilling over the lace cups of her bra. His hands bunched in the hem of her blouse at her back, tunneling beneath her sweater, then beneath the silk camisole she wore underneath it. At the first brush of his palm on her naked back, over the little hummingbird she'd had inked there when she'd freed herself from the past, a plaintive little moan chirped from her in a clear message of want.

She was pretty sure he understood the sound by the way his shaft strained against his jeans, strained against her belly. She tucked her hips closer, pressed herself nearer that fiery source of male heat.

His hands traveled up her back with the same slow restraint he'd always shown around her and she wondered vaguely if she'd ever be so fortunate to see this man unleash the kind of raw want that she had tonight. She tried to lean back to gauge his expression, to see if he wanted this as badly as she did, but he held her fast with his hands, keeping her breasts pressed to his chest while he unfastened hooks and lowered straps and finally cupped the soft weights in his hand.

And somehow that was answer enough.

Her hands stilled on his shoulders, her whole body tensed with anticipating his touch on the taut peaks of her breasts. The teasing feel of her silk camisole on the tight points was nothing compared to what Sean's touch would be like.

Now it was his turn to lean back, to take in the sight of her with her sweater falling off her shoulder, her camisole stretched taut against the breasts he cupped in his hands. Her whole body was buzzing, humming, tingling and he seemed to sense that as he drew out the moment, looking at her.

Then, bending over her, he closed his lips on one tight peak through the fabric. The moist heat of the kiss sent a shudder through her as she arched, offering him total access. His tongue laved the point through the silk, creating a damp spot and heightening the sensation of his tongue directly on her. At her needy whimper, he kissed the other nipple in the same way, teasing her into a frenzy of erratic breathing and restless hands.

She wanted more. Much more. Her needs had been ignored too long for her to remember the finesse of seduction but she wanted to seduce Sean, to please him and make him want more. She palmed the length of him through his jeans, testing the breadth of an impressive erection.

"Bedroom." His muffled word was his only explanation for lifting her off her feet and swinging her into his arms, but it seemed sufficient.

She would have gladly let him take her on the floor of his living room except that she imagined a man might keep his condoms by his bed as opposed to his coffee table.

And she liked being carried this way since it put her breasts at feasting level for him and he used the short trip to suck her deep into his mouth.

She felt the power of that kiss all the way to her core, her hips tilting in helpless response. Her foot grazed the door frame as he angled them into his bedroom, and the small jolt helped her stave off the orgasm that threatened. He hadn't even touched her between her thighs yet and already she was wound tight enough for mind-numbing release.

"Sorry," he whispered as he stalked past a huge wardrobe and a media center toward the back of the room where his sleigh bed loomed high off the hardwood floor. Everything in the room felt big and masculine from the stark, chunky furnishings to the steely muscles binding her to him.

"My toe doesn't hurt half as much as other places, believe me." She'd barely felt the knock against her foot, whereas the ache in her womb taunted her with a persistence that wouldn't go away without his help.

Grinning, he lowered her onto his bed.

"We can't have you in pain." He smoothed a palm across her belly, his pinky finger dipping into the waistband of her jeans to torment her even more. "I promise I can take care of that."

Donata struggled between the desire to simply lie back and allow him to have his wicked way with her—preferably as soon as possible—and the need to pull off his clothes. She finally compromised by keeping her hips glued to the bed where he was touching her and giving her hands free rein to tug off his shirt.

She unveiled his abs first, an impressive wall of muscles carved into six neat squares. Breaking her own code to stay still, she couldn't resist leaning forward to run her tongue along the ridge of those muscles, defining each one with a slow lick.

His low groan pleased her, the heat from his skin making her shiver in anticipation.

"I don't think I can wait." She sat up abruptly, figuring if he wasn't used to her blunt-speaking ways by now, there would be no point proceeding with this encounter anyhow.

"Patience is overrated," he agreed, reaching into the nightstand drawer and coming back with a foil packet he tossed on the bed. "I'll take all the time in the world later—after we take the edge off."

Gotta love practical men. Passionate men.

Reaching for the snap on her jeans, she started to wriggle out of the denim at the same time he removed his completely. He'd been commando underneath, so this new view distracted her from her own efforts.

Men might not be beautiful the way women were beautiful, but he looked damn good to her right now. His shaft rose high and straight, the darkly engorged head calling to her fingertips urgently.

She transplanted her touch to his erection, her hand encircling him while her thumb traced the head. Thankfully, Sean's nimble fingers took over the task of peeling off her remaining clothes, his fingers hesitating only briefly to circle the tattooed rose on her hip before he tugged off her lacy red thong.

She hoped he didn't have nosy neighbors because the shades hadn't been drawn on the two windows near the media center. Fortunately, it was dark in his bedroom, with only the streetlights below to illuminate them as they faced off in total nakedness.

The feel of cool air against her nether regions sent a warning spasm through her whole body, a precursor of the way she'd fly apart in a million pieces soon.

"I'm not kidding, Sean." She wrapped her hand around his hip to pull him down to the bed with her. "It's been a really long time for me."

She needed him *now*.

He didn't ask her to spell out *how* long, but maybe he could already guess given how devoted she'd been to her work.

"Just one quick taste." His gaze was fastened to her bikini line and she was grateful she'd kept herself neatly groomed despite the total lack of bedroom action for four years.

"No." Another spasm threatened and she squeezed her legs together to ward it off until he was ready to join her. "Please. I want this first release to happen when I have you inside me."

The admission revealed a need for intimacy she hadn't meant to show him, but she hadn't known how much she wanted that kind of completion until the words fell out of her mouth.

She reached for the condom to facilitate her wishes and he pulled her to the edge of the bed at the same time while he remained standing over her. He cradled the backs of her thighs, lifting them, lifting *her* against the hard heat of him. She tore open the packet and sheathed him with trembling fingers while he smoothed his hands up to her bottom to cup her.

How could she have forgotten how deeply personal this moment could be? She stared at him in the reflected glow of city lights that cast the room in shadows. Modern media often depicted sex with such casualness that she'd almost bought into the idea a man and woman could fulfill one another's sexual needs without entangling themselves in deeper emotions.

But just now she realized that would never be true for her. There would be hell to pay for her heart, her feelings, her good mental health after this night with Sean, but she wouldn't have stopped now for anything. The need inside her twisted painfully and she raised her hips to take him.

She bit her lip to take her mind off the incredible pleasure since she was determined to have him fully inside her before she let herself go. She'd always liked to maintain a certain amount of control in the bedroom, but it was becoming impossible with this man.

"Am I hurting you?" He paused to stroke her thighs and he bent forward to kiss her eyelids.

The tenderness inherent in that gesture threatened to swamp her with emotions. She prayed for some control, some sense of restraint behind passions that could easily overwhelm her.

"It's too good for words," she admitted, her breath coming in and out at high speed as she held herself utterly still, mesmerized by powerful sensations. "I'm just trying to stall the inevitable."

He studied her through half-lowered lashes, his assessing gaze missing nothing, seeing deep inside her to raw emotions she didn't quite know how to veil. Sean saw too much.

But just when she felt her most vulnerable, when she came the closest to weeping with hunger and need and longing, he pushed her legs farther apart and seated himself fully inside her.

"Don't hold back." He spoke directly into her ear as he withdrew from her slowly and then repeated the breath-stealing thrust inside her. "I want to see you unravel for me, Donata. Only for me."

He licked his thumb and then centered the damp pad on her clit as he repeated the thrust. The sweet pressure at the center of her combined with the thick heat between her legs had her spiraling out of control in no time, her shout of fulfillment echoing throughout the room and maybe the whole apartment.

Tiny spasms fluttered over her skin as deep, lush contractions squeezed her insides as wave after wave of sensual nirvana washed through her whole body. She squeezed *him,* too, her feminine muscles clenching around him until he had no choice but to join her in the mindless abyss of endless pleasure.

Words escaped her as they lay in silence afterward. Simply breathing seemed a monumental task since she swore she could have died from the thrill of rediscovering passion. No, not rediscovering. This was better than anything she'd ever felt before so she seemed to be unearthing something all new and wonderful.

Assuming she didn't let it cloud her judgment.

Breathe in. Breathe out.

Her mind floated away to half sleep and she knew she shouldn't have been so utterly selfish, putting her needs first. But she'd been powerless to thwart the demands of her body that had been so long denied.

Still, as her breathing finally slowed down to soft hitches, Donata wondered how she would ever resurrect her facade of cool distance with this man after a night that caused her to come so undone in more ways than one.

6

WHEN SEAN FIRST MET Donata, she'd been the outspoken girlfriend of a gangster. Mouthy, haughty and fiercely protective of her man if any cops came around to give Sergio a hard time.

But as much as he abhorred Sergio's crimes, Sean had always found something to admire about Donata, even before he knew she was only staying with the guy to help bust him. Maybe the rogue cop within him had responded to her fearlessness bordering on recklessness, the devil-may-care spirit that allowed her to lie to protect her own at any cost.

Sean had thought that woman was long dead and buried—or maybe she'd only been an act pulled off by a woman bent on revenge. But after tonight, he knew that fearless, borderline reckless Donata was alive and well and more appealing than ever. The fiery, passionate woman she'd always been had steeled into a resourceful, determined woman he could truly admire on many levels.

Now, lying beside her in the middle of the night, he stroked a kinky strand of blond hair from her forehead and marveled that she had fallen asleep in his bed and in his arms. She'd rallied after they made love the first time, making noises about leaving so they could salvage a working relationship without worrying sex would confuse things. But he'd talked her around. Hell, who was he kidding? He'd touched her and teased her until she saw his point of view on the subject.

The second time they'd come together had been even more incredible than the first. And that was saying something because it had taken him half an hour to catch his breath after the first time. Donata held nothing back in bed, a sharp contrast from the way she conducted herself in her day-to-day life. At work, she hid her earthy side under conservative suits and clipped cop-speak. But when she set aside those restraints— Well, damn. He was still seeing stars from the aftermath.

"I can't afford to mess up my career." Donata's sudden soft words surprised him since he thought she'd been sleeping.

"You're not going to hurt your career." He didn't know what she was worried about since she'd put in a boatload of unpaid overtime already in the days since they'd met again. "You're working your butt off on this case."

"I know, but it doesn't feel right since I've hardly seen Mick this week." Her eyes fluttered open as she tightened her hold on the sheet. "With his daughter giving him the runaround and her mother not putting her foot down about it, Mick is stuck playing the bad guy. He's just so anxious to keep Katie safe that his mind isn't on work."

She was silent for a moment, staring down at the assortments of rings on her fingers until she met his gaze again.

"Doesn't his ex-wife get how damaging it is for Katie to have no limits?"

Donata's question helped the pieces fall into place for Sean as he realized how much she must identify with the girl who hadn't been given boundaries.

"How damaging is it?" He didn't mean to pry, per se. But he was curious about Donata's life. Her past. What led her to shack up with a gangster as a teenager?

"Sorry. I don't believe in pawning off my hard-luck story to make it sound like I had the worst child-hood in history." She propped herself up in his bed, drawing her knees up close to her chest while she tucked the tawny-colored blankets underneath her chin. "I've heard tales a hell of a lot worse since I've been on the force and I'm sure you did, too. I just wish so-called enlightened parents would get a clue that their open-minded approach to raising kids is a one-way ticket to disaster for a teenager."

"I'm *asking* to hear your story, Donata, because we're friends. That's not the same as you pawning it off on me." Although, he admitted to himself, he admired her even more for not using her past as an excuse for her choices. He liked that bottom-line mentality she had that suggested she wasn't one to pass the buck.

Staring down over her knees, she tucked the thermal blanket between her toes.

"My mom took off on my dad before I was ten. I loved her, I missed her, I blamed myself even though I knew my father wasn't a picnic to live with. Blaming me seemed easier than blaming her since, you know, she was my mom."

Sitting up in the bed, he wrapped an arm around her while she spoke, wishing she'd been raised with a little more tenderness. What parent walked away from her own kid?

"And before you commiserate about how much that sucked, trust me, in my neighborhood it wasn't such a bad fate. I had friends whose mothers beat them or who sold their daughter's virginity to a drug dealer to support a meth habit. I had a Disney upbringing by comparison." She glared at him in the shadowed light of the room.

Sean got the message—she wanted him to stay quiet while she told the story she clearly didn't share very often. And so he didn't say a word, merely rubbed her bare back, his fingers trailing over her spine to trace an outline over the hummingbird fluttering just above her hips.

"Anyway, my dad was a hippie throwback, a guy who believed in free love and open marriage and no locks on his front door. He didn't care where I went as long as I was 'finding myself.' It didn't take many years for me to realize that I'd find myself dead or raped in my own bed if he didn't install locks on our doors. We got robbed three times in a year before I left. The last time, I woke up to some bug-eyed dude on a heroin trip who figured he'd steal my first time from me since there was virtually nothing else in the house to be stolen by then."

Memories of his sister's encounter with a molester flooded him with anger and he didn't stand a chance of staying quiet any longer.

"Son of a—"

"Nothing happened," she explained quickly, shaking her head before he let loose the full gamut of expletives and fury he felt on her behalf. "As luck would have it, I'd eaten an apple that night before bed and I still had the knife that I used to peel it on the nightstand. Joe Bug-Eyes got a hell of a surprise when he tried to take my clothes off."

She released a pent-up breath and he had the feeling there was more to this story.

"But you said he was tripping. Did he even feel it when you stabbed him?" Sean had seen guys single-handedly battle three cops when they were flying too high.

"The guy raised the roof with screaming at me. Half the neighborhood ended up in my bedroom that night, including Sergio from down the street who—for all I know—was the bastard who sold the drugs to my attacker." She shook her head and Sean could see the disillusionment in her eyes when she turned to look at him. "But at the time, he looked clean and strong and well dressed. To a sixteen-year-old kid, that's a hell of an endorsement for a guy's character. It didn't take long for me to decide life with Sergio— and four walls with locking doors—would be a lot safer than living under my father's roof."

"I'm sure it was. For all of Serg's faults, I imagine he wouldn't let anyone else touch you." Which was more than she could say for her own father.

"The joys of dysfunction." She lifted a halfhearted smile in his direction. "I learned in therapy that he was a surrogate father figure, a fact that totally grossed me out, but it ultimately gave me enough distance from him to start seeing him for the criminal he really was. Although, now that I think about it, the fact that he took a mistress in the later years helped me feel pretty distant from him, too."

"Rosie Gillespie. I remember the flap because her photos were posted on the same Internet Web site as my sister's. I questioned her way back when about that but she made it clear she didn't want any part of cops." Sean didn't mention that she'd also claimed Sergio as her protector. Not that it scared off Sean, but the woman had made it plain she considered the police her enemies. "You said you were in therapy before you left Sergio?"

He'd always imagined Donata had straightened her life out more recently—when she'd signed on to the force.

"Aside from his criminal pursuits, he used to get

a real paycheck from an auto body shop and the benefits were great. The HMO let me visit a shrink after I made a case that I was like a common-law wife after I turned twenty." She twisted a curly lock around one finger. "I got out of the house by letting Serg think I needed my hair done every week."

She winked at him, and he caught a mental picture of what she must have been like then, faking vanity to get real help for herself.

"You're amazing." He wondered how many twenty-year-olds could untangle the myriad of clauses in an HMO well enough to obtain free counseling, let alone have enough self-awareness to want to undertake such a feat.

"Hardly. I'm a scrapper at heart. I just cover it up better now that I've learned skills for professional behavior." Yawning, she tipped her head sideways to rest on her knees.

"You must be tired." He wanted to hold her while she slept, to protect her for a few hours to make up for the way she'd had to look out for herself for most of her life.

And wasn't that a surprise? He'd never felt called to play the role of guardian for a woman—except his sister—outside his old police work. Yet this fiercely independent female had him thinking about all the ways he could step into the line of fire for her.

"I should get home before I can't keep my eyes open any longer."

He didn't want her to go. He even contemplated

using the case to convince her to stay. While he had a few other ideas about where to take the investigation next, he was trying not to step on her toes so they could both do their jobs.

"A court order could force the store to release the credit card numbers of whoever bought the equipment to send to my fake ID. If Sara Chapman received her webcam equipment the same way, you'd have good leverage to obtain the order."

Had he thought he could keep his opinions to himself? Dumb ass. Just when he'd successfully stifled one suggestion on her case, another one came flying out his mouth.

A startled expression crossed her face at his sudden change of topic. "I'll talk to Mick about that and I'm going to have to face Sergio if I want any resolution on how my photos are getting passed around." Donata untucked the blanket from her toes. "I know he's probably the driving force behind the move to discredit me, but since he's in jail, there has to be someone else doing the dirty work."

"You're not going to see that dirtball by yourself." Her partner would show up for something like that, right? Sean didn't appreciate the way Mick's attention was fracturing when Donata needed him most.

"I don't know." She slid out of bed, her naked body making his mouth water in spite of the tense nature of their conversation. "I might be more effective in wresting information from him if I go alone. After all those counseling sessions I sat through to untwine my head, I'm pretty good at asking probing, open-ended questions that initiate dialogue."

She put her clothes on in quick order and something about that hasty speed made him wonder if she already regretted getting close to him. The realization pinched more than he would have guessed.

"You're not racing out of here just to put tonight in the past, are you?"

His question must have caught her off guard because she spun on her heel and stared at him with the deer-in-the-headlights freeze for all of two seconds before she darted out the door, only to return with her purse and her coat. She jammed her arms into the sleeves of the jacket, her movements abrupt.

Unsteady?

"Honestly, you know as well as I do that sleeping together while working together doesn't usually make for success on either front. But that's not why I'm leaving." She tugged the strap of her leather purse onto her shoulder and then approached the bed.

She was silent for so long, he had to nudge her along.

"So what gives?" He stroked the back of her hand, hoping he hadn't blown it with her when he'd barely gotten the chance to know her.

"You'll think it sounds stupid, and it probably is. After I helped send Serg to jail, I promised myself I wouldn't wake up to another man's head on my pillow unless he was The One."

It took him a minute to fully digest the inherent romanticism in the sentiment, a fact that surprised him coming from a woman he considered to be street-smart and tough.

"Technically, this is my pillow." He tugged the rumpled headrest closer to the edge of the bed. "So I don't think you'd be breaking the rules."

"Thanks, Sean. But since you're already the first man I've slept with in four years, I don't think you want to add that kind of pressure to the mix."

And without another word, she was gone, leaving Sean to wonder if he'd already waded in over his head where Donata was concerned.

"SO DOES Mrs. Chapman think the boyfriend planted the webcam in Sara's bedroom for his own benefit, or does she have reason to believe he planned to sell the footage?" Donata made an effort to focus on the conversation with her partner the next afternoon even though thoughts of Sean and their night together were creeping into her head at every turn.

She wondered if she had that goofy, good sex afterglow today. She knew she shouldn't place too much emphasis on what had happened with Sean when she needed to keep her guard up around him, but that hadn't stopped her from reliving every delicious moment in his bed and in his arms.

But while she was glowing like a teenager, Mick looked as though he hadn't slept in a week as he shuffled through the notes on his desk. His hair stuck up in the back and the two cups of sugar-loaded java she'd made for him hadn't come close to erasing the lines around his eyes.

"She doesn't have anything concrete. The first time I talked to her she seemed to think the boyfriend—" he scanned the notes "—Terrance Russell, was a great guy. But apparently since the case broke, Terrance dumped Sara and both the Chapman women are upset about it."

"Upset?" She'd thought he hesitated over the word choice so she tracked back to it.

"More mad than you'd expect over a high school breakup, but maybe that's because they're convinced the boyfriend planted the webcams. They sort of hounded me about when I'd arrest the kid."

"You think they conspired to direct the blame now that mother and daughter have had time to discuss it? Maybe Sara put her own webcams in place and doesn't want to admit she liked giving the kid a free show, so now that he dumped her, she'll get even?" It was possible, and the girl might not realize the bigger blame rested with whoever made the Web images into a film for profitable distribution.

"I don't know. I've had a tough time tracking down this Terrance kid and maybe he's ducking me because he's guilty as hell. I'm just telling you there was some definite angling going on at the Chapman household."

Nodding, Donata understood how it felt to be betrayed by the guy you'd given yourself to. Some anger and resentment—and yes, a desire for revenge—were all common reactions.

Donata refused to think about the fact that she'd set herself up for betrayal all over again last night by sleeping with Sean. Not that Sean had anything in common with lowlife Serg, but even a prince among men could break a woman's heart and Donata knew if she wasn't careful, she could wind up hurt.

The thought helped her focus on the case. She wouldn't let any more girls make the same mistakes Sara Chapman had.

"I've got a lot of electronic leads I'm following up and then I thought I'd interview Sergio about the pictures to see if he gives anything away." She hesitated, biting the end of her pen as she debated how to tell her partner the latest on that front. "My photos are on the Internet now, so it made zero sense to blackmail me. I'm sending the link information to the tech guys and maybe they can trace who posted it."

"Oh, shit."

"Tell me about it." She'd been stripped of all her defenses last night—personal and professional. There was no place to hide the vulnerable girl she'd once been. Her mistakes were available to view for anyone with a computer and an Internet connection.

And, oh God, the roiling in her stomach told her she needed to resurrect some boundaries soon. Now. Immersing herself in the investigation seemed like the wisest solution.

"You don't need to submit the link as part of the case file, Donata." Mick's eyes looked fully alert for the first time all day as he reached over his desk to slap one big palm across the manila folder she'd brought into the precinct today.

Phones rang and officers laughed, yelled and cursed all around them, but for a moment, she and Mick shared a moment of intense staring, each trying to fathom where the other was coming from.

"Why wouldn't I share this information?" She knew why she didn't want to, but she didn't understand how holding back could be ethical.

"Have someone else track it. Jesus, woman, let Sean track it. He's made a small fortune tackling Internet crimes for corporate execs the last few years. It's been his bread and butter to support himself while he pursues his own personal crusade. He's got great resources for this."

"How do you know what kinds of cases Sean takes?" She'd been under the impression they'd only just met. And why didn't she know about Sean's area of specialty?

Still, an idea sparked in the back of her mind for bringing their perp to justice.

"The longer you stick around here, the more you realize what a small world the NYPD is. There are thirty-nine thousand of us in all, but those numbers narrow quite a bit when you're looking only at detectives and, in particular, detectives who've worked in Manhattan." A tired grin brightened his weary face. "Wait until your first stakeout. You'll realize how well gossip and doughnuts go together when you're dog-ass tired and want to go home. You'll know the scoop on everyone who ever walked through this precinct."

"Somebody else might get away with not filing a piece of evidence, Mick, even if it's peripheral. But I've got a background that makes a lot of people around here uncomfortable."

He shook his head and scooped up his notes.

"I've seen the arrests you've made, Casale, and I know if you were a guy I'd say you had balls of steel on the street. When are you going to bring a little more of those guts into the precinct with you?"

She hadn't expected a response that bordered on angry, but then she knew her partner wasn't at his best today. She felt bad she hadn't gotten around to asking about his daughter.

He rounded her desk on his way out to continue his two cents that was quickly adding up to ten.

"It's no different in here than it is out there. You hold your head up and let the shit slide right off you or they'll bring you down to their level until the brass is filling your shoes with another rookie next fall."

He stalked toward the front doors, ignoring the handful of greetings on his way through the desks and causing a few heads to turn toward her as if to see the source of the problem.

She didn't appreciate Mick's tone or his delivery, but she trusted his take on police politics. So she politely flipped off one of the younger guys who cast a censuring look her way and turned her attention to her own computer.

While she debated what to do about reporting her online photos, she was pretty sure she heard a couple of the older guys laughing while they took turns razzing the officer she'd been rude to. At least no one was glaring at her anymore.

Maybe the time had come to stop praying for acceptance here. She had enough on her plate without worrying about her popularity in the 10th precinct. Because after a sleepless night at home, she'd figured out the best way to bring down the adult filmmaker passing off private webcam footage as reality porn would be to go undercover with herself as bait.

7

"HELL NO."

Sean didn't know how else to respond to Donata's suggestion the next day as they drove out to the Hamptons. He'd agreed to go with her when she said she was headed to Long Island since he'd assumed she wanted to interview Sara Chapman's boyfriend or some other suspects in the case.

But then she'd spelled out an insane plan to gather evidence against the perp planting webcams by making herself a potential target.

"Don't shoot it down until you hear how limited our options are at this point." Donata never took her eyes off the road as she steered her no-frills Ford sedan over Interstate 495 toward glitzy South Hampton, far from the more residential Massapequa where Sara Chapman lived. Traffic was light on a weekday, the commuters already safely at work while Donata and Sean made their way east.

"Your options aren't as limited as you think." He didn't know how to break the mix of good news/bad news to her since she probably wouldn't appreciate his sleight of hand with her online photo.

"What do you mean?" She did turn to glance at him then, her eyebrows knit in worry.

Guilt rattled him for all of a second since he hated the idea of being another guy who let her down, but damn it, this was for the best.

"I gathered a good piece of information yesterday but I unearthed it in the course of taking down your picture from that Web site." There. He'd admitted it. Even as he waited for her anger, he felt a weight off his shoulders. "I made a copy of the relevant pages with a time stamp so you can still submit them as evidence, but I had a tech guy reroute the link to a self-help site for pedophiles."

Her short bark of laughter wasn't exactly full of good humor. More like a shout of disbelief.

"You took down the picture you knew I was going to submit as evidence?" Accusation permeated the words.

"Yes, but I knew the way I gathered the evidence would protect it in court without making it continually available. I've had good luck with Internet crime cases at my firm, and I know what will hold up in front of a judge. There was no need for you to let that image stay live on the site if you were uncomfortable with it."

Seeing that picture had made him want to throw a blanket around her naked self. It didn't matter that he also wanted to unveil her in private. No guy should see this woman in the altogether without earning the right to her bed first.

"I'm not sure what I think about those tactics

when I clearly asked you to let me handle it." Her fingers gripped the steering wheel harder, her knuckles clenched. "What evidence did you find?"

"For starters, we found some file coding associated with the photo that matches part of the screen name for one of the people who sent me a webcam."

"I don't get it. What kind of file coding?"

"The name someone used to save the digital image. Part of the name contains the letters f-s-t-g-r-l-z and one of the donators to my online wish list was 'fastgirlz.' Seemed a close enough match to warrant further investigation."

They turned off the interstate onto a smaller highway heading south toward the coast. The houses were a hell of a lot bigger here, with more green space. Some snow remained in patches on a few of the lawns, but the weather today was clear and cool.

"You said that was just for starters?"

"I checked my record log for sites I've visited in the past year, and Fast Girlz productions was a site I hit five months ago. It's gone now, but my notes at the time were that the girls looked close enough to legal age that I wouldn't bother checking into them. Obviously, I didn't realize the videos they advertised were probably made without the subjects' knowledge."

"You didn't make a copy of that Web page the way you did with the site my picture was posted on?"

"Just so happens, I did." He waved the folder in his lap, damn proud of himself for keeping good notes. "Turns out there are benefits to obsessive vigilantism."

"I never said you were obsessive." She frowned and didn't seem to realize he was kidding. But then, Donata seemed like a woman well-accustomed to being on guard all the time. Maybe her sense of humor had fallen to the wayside the past few years.

Her looks sure as hell hadn't. Once again today her lips were outlined in a perfect red Cupid's bow that made him want to kiss her and mess up that sleek veneer of hers.

"I know. But the vigilante accusation hit home. Maybe I'm just trying to assure myself the efforts have been worth it." He'd been so determined not to miss any criminal business that the case had been open a hell of a long time after they'd caught the guy who molested his sister. Sean had turned the hunt for online predators into a four-year mission. He recognized the time had come to start tossing guys in jail.

"Thank you for opening your files to me." She paused as she pulled up to a T intersection. "And although I wish you'd talked to me about taking down my picture first, I am glad it's gone."

She took a left on a road that ran along the coast, the view of the water occasionally obscured by tall trees and landscaping or privacy hedges, but he glimpsed the ocean waves now and then as they sped past one spectacular property after another.

"Sorry. It's been a long time since I've had to worry about checking my methods with anyone else and I guess I got out of the habit." It was one of the coolest perks in his private investigator work. No jumping through someone else's hoops.

"That's okay. I'm starting to see the wisdom of occasionally forging my own path at work, which is why I'm going through with using myself as bait."

She slowed down near a sign for a bed-and-breakfast and put on her turn signal.

"That's different." He couldn't let her do this when there had to be ten other ways to make arrests on the case.

"It's not different." She pulled into the small parking lot that held four other cars and turned off the engine. "I've got the best connections to bring down whoever's behind this ring. If some of the people behind this are friends of Sergio's they'll be all the more likely to screw up in their haste to get even with me. It's a perfect plan and nothing you say is going to make me change my mind."

THEY DROVE ALL THE WAY back to Manhattan that night after Donata checked into the bed-and-breakfast—alone. She wanted the word to spread in the small Southampton community that she was back and staying in the small B&B in the hopes that who-ever wanted to make trouble for her would jump at the chance to plant cameras around her hotel room, using the prominent laptop on the desk as a source to hook up illegal webcams.

What the perp wouldn't know was that she and

Sean had hidden a smaller, wireless laptop in the closet and connected two webcams to that device so they could see who came into the hotel room when she wasn't there. That last part was Sean's idea and Donata had to admit, it made the ruse safer. She just hoped they'd covered their butts every way possible to avoid any chance of their guy pleading entrapment.

But after going over and over their plans on the ride home, she still had nearly an hour of sitting quietly next to Sean in the intimate confines of the smaller car she'd bought for its gas mileage rather than roominess. By the time she pulled onto the West Side Highway, she was antsy to break out of the car so the cool air could blow over her overheated body.

"You're going back to my place?" He sprawled in the seat beside her, his knee protruding far enough into her personal space to make her aware of him and how long it had been since he'd touched her.

Not that she was keeping track of those forty-two hours.

"I thought I'd drop you off. Save you cab fare from the Upper East Side." She assumed he'd want to go home at this hour—well after dinner. "Would you rather I stop off somewhere else?"

"No. My place has good karma for us."

His voice carried as much meaning as his words, the tone low and laced with the same longing she'd been feeling all day.

And while she couldn't deny a rush of relief that he wanted her as much as she wanted him, she didn't know how much more time she could risk with him without getting her heart stomped on.

"You're awfully quiet on that subject," he observed lightly when she didn't respond.

"I've never been one to jump into relationships lightly—contrary to my decision to move in with a gangster when I was a teenager." Would she ever be okay with that part of her life? Mick had told her she needed to stop feeling guilty about it, and she wanted to. But how did you go about ignoring your emotions?

"I guessed as much since you told me you haven't been with anyone else since they locked up Alteri." He reached through the darkness inside the vehicle to slide his hand under her hair and massage the back of her neck.

He didn't say any more about the matter, leaving it up to her to try and express a knotted bunch of worries that she didn't completely understand herself. Why couldn't she be one of those women who just enjoyed sex for sex's sake without all the accompanying tenderness?

"I pride myself on being hard-nosed in a lot of areas of my life, Sean, but sex isn't one of them. I…enjoyed the other night. But I can't make love in a recreational way because that's just not me. I mean, one night to take the edge off after it had been so many years—that I can forgive myself for. But I'm not the kind of person who can separate my feelings from sex."

"And you don't have feelings for me." The warmth in his voice had vanished and it took Donata a minute to understand how he had interpreted her words.

"Uh—no. That's not quite what I meant." She hadn't intended to hurt him and it caught her off guard to think maybe she had. Could he have feelings for *her* so soon? "I just didn't get the impression that you were looking for anything more from me than what we shared last time, and frankly, I'm not interested in messing around just for the sake of great orgasms."

"Damn, woman, you sure can cut to the chase."

"I'm just trying to be honest." Something that became more and more difficult the deeper she got involved with Sean since owning up to her emotions didn't come easily. Better to erect a few boundaries now. She slid into a parking space on his street about half a block away from his building. "I really value that from people in my life these days, and I hold myself accountable for dealing as squarely with others as I'd want them to be with me."

He leaned over the console to shut off the ignition, dropping one hand onto her knee while he fingered the back of her neck with the other.

"But you haven't given me a chance to be honest with you since you left in a hurry the other night and all our time since then has been dedicated to the investigation. You can't possibly know what I'm thinking about us when you don't give me any time with you outside of work."

Nervous tension threaded through her at the suggestion of a heart-to-heart and she didn't think she was ready to handle wading through the aftermath of what they'd done. Could she afford to be *that* honest when she wasn't even sure what she wanted these days?

"I'm not at my best tonight after the long drive." She knew it was a weak excuse, but they had worked their tails off to set up the room at the bed-and-breakfast and to make appearances around town to help spread the word Donata Casale was back in Sergio's old stomping ground.

Who would take the bait? One of his friends whose pockets were empty now that Sergio was in jail? One of his mistresses who coveted Donata's position as his live-in?

"Fine. So we don't attempt some drawn-out discussion tonight. But you can't shut me out without giving me a chance to talk to you." His hand slid up her thigh with pulse-hammering effect and she found herself wishing she drove a car with a bench seat.

She nodded jerkily, her body unwilling to move anywhere that Sean wasn't steering her. His hand paused at her hip and then slid under her jacket and the blouse beneath it to graze the bare skin at her waist. He curved his other arm around her shoulders, drawing her closer to his side of the car and the temptation of his mouth.

"And until you give me that chance to talk, I'm going to provide you with a few things to think about."

He slanted his lips over hers in a heated melding of mouths, his tongue slick and hot as he dipped inside for a thorough taste. The intimate act his kiss mimicked was suddenly imprinted on her brain, reminding her of all the experiences they hadn't gotten to share in their short time together when she'd been wound so tightly she couldn't last through the most decadent of sexual acts.

And how did he know that this blatant kiss would remind her so keenly?

A sharp pang of want shot through her as he lifted her over the console to settle her in his lap. They weren't exactly in a position of privacy here since anyone on the street would be able to see them through the windshield. But it was dark out and she'd parked on the opposite end of the street from the coffee shop so there wasn't much foot traffic.

She wound her arms around him as he shifted sideways in his seat to give her more leg room. A taller woman might not have enough head clearance on his lap, but she couldn't have been any more delectably positioned on his muscular thigh with his mouth still planted on hers.

The temperature in the car climbed a few degrees as she stroked his hair in silent encouragement. She didn't want this kiss to end, no matter what logical protests her rational brain concocted. The fire inside could take charge for a few minutes and kissing eliminated the need for thinking.

And it seemed like she waved goodbye to practical worries just in time since his hand on her waist skimmed higher beneath her blouse to brush the underside of one silk-covered breast. Her yelp of pleasure filled the car interior. His thumb stroked upward over the fabric to tease the peak quickly tightening at his touch.

His tortured groan was followed by a soft curse as he broke away.

"That's probably enough to think about for one night." He allowed himself one last soft pinch to her aching nipple before he slid his hand out from under her shirt. Donata felt the teasing last stroke all the way to her womb.

Her heart tripped in its rapid beat as she contemplated a night alone stretching in front of her when Sean so clearly wanted her to come upstairs. With her thighs settled so snugly across his lap, she knew exactly how much he wanted her with him tonight.

"It's *too* much to think about," she protested, the nerve endings in her lips buzzing pleasantly from his kiss. She gathered fists full of his T-shirt, and rocked closer to him, wondering how a man could start something so delicious if he had no intention of finishing it.

Of finishing her.

He wrapped his hands around her hips to still her.

"I only meant to remind you how hot it would be."

"Looks like you reminded me a little too well." She took a deep breath to steady herself and only succeeded in pressing her breasts more firmly against his chest. And, Lord have mercy, that felt good. "Do you care to tell me how I'm supposed to sleep tonight?"

He kissed her again, his tongue sliding over hers and melting all resistance until he pulled away again.

"Damned if I know. I sure as hell won't be sleeping." His breath came fast and his heart pounded manically beneath hers.

Or was that her heart drumming incessantly?

"Maybe one more time wouldn't hurt." In the back of her mind, she probably knew better, but what choice did she have when her only other option was to spontaneously combust? "Isn't sex a scientific need? Right after food and shelter, it's sex, right?"

He levered open the car door then and spun her around so she could put her feet on the pavement.

"It is for us, apparently." He grabbed her keys before locking the car door behind him. He took her hand and tugged her up the street toward his building. "Who would have thought two such practical people would turn into raving sex fiends when faced with the prospect of a little necking?"

She hastened her step to keep up with him, not sure if she was making good decisions anymore but unable to walk away from him. From this.

She noticed his hands fumbled on the keys before he got the locks turned, the grim set to his jaw indicating how seriously he took this. Did he feel compelled to be with her the same way she felt compelled to be with him?

God, she hoped so. Her desire for Sean was driven purely by choice. She could have been with any number of men over the past few years, her life filled with honorable guys ever since the day she'd entered the police academy. But she hadn't wanted anyone until Sean.

And, if she was honest with herself, maybe that had made life easier for her since avoiding men had freed her from the need to trust her romantic judgment again.

"Come on in." He drew her into the building and shut the door behind them, but he spun her around before she got to the stairs. "I can't go any farther without another taste of you."

And then he was kissing her again, backing her into the banister in the middle of the foyer. She welcomed the hard press of the polished handrail into her back, the only thing keeping her on her feet when he applied such devastating skill to ravishing her mouth. Her senses. His fingers walked up the outside of her thighs, making her wish her slacks would fall away so he could touch her bare skin. Or better yet, she wished his jeans would fall away so she could touch *his* bare skin.

"Upstairs," she murmured, reaching for the handrail to steady herself for the climb to his apartment. "I can't do this without unraveling."

He pulled away, his hazel gaze sizzling her insides with a look of pure fire. She would have given him everything right here if he'd kissed her again, so she started up the steps on quivering legs, knowing they needed to get behind closed doors soon. His frustrated growl made her smile as he followed her, and the trip up two flights was punctuated with occasional caresses on the backs of her calves, her thighs, her butt, from hands he couldn't keep to himself.

By the time they reached his apartment door, she gladly took a small measure of sensual revenge while he unbolted the locks. She licked his cheek and unbuckled his belt with slow deliberation while he worked the keys, her hand hovering over his zipper.

When he opened the door to his apartment, she knew there was no turning back. And even though her hunger for him had her stepping over the threshold toward an enticing possible future, in the back of her mind she couldn't help but wonder if the ugly truth of her past followed hot on her heels.

8

SEAN SLAMMED THE DOOR so hard the windows rattled.

He didn't know how he'd managed to lure this incredible woman to his apartment, but he wasn't about to question fate when it burned red-hot and tempting right in front of him. She slipped off her shoes on his front mat, a simple act of familiarity that turned something over inside him. A woman's bare feet shouldn't turn him on this much, but knowing he'd won Donata over tonight, knowing the fire between them had roared past her defenses to land her here against her practical intentions—that turned him on a whole hell of a lot.

"Happy to see me, Mr. Beringer?" She slid out of her jacket as she wandered closer, her breasts straining the fabric of her blouse when she arched her arms back to let the blazer fall free.

He realized he was grinning and damned if he could stop himself. He felt as though he'd just won the lottery.

"You'd put a smile on any guy's face." He bracketed her waist with his hands and drew her to him, his thumbs circling her hip bones above the top of low-slung pants.

"That's where you're wrong." She slid her hands up his shirt slowly, taking her time. "I don't put a smile on very many male faces at all, so when I do, you can consider yourself sort of special."

When she tugged the shirt off his shoulders, she pressed forward enough to brush her breasts over his bare chest and he got the distinct impression she was going to pay him back for his aggressive kisses in the car.

"Special isn't quite the word for how I'm feeling." He wanted to lay her back and take possession of this barefooted woman who looked so sure of herself and so comfortable in his home. He wanted to feel the primal satisfaction that came with lying on top of her, easing her legs apart and making her his.

Instead, she unzipped his jeans and lowered his boxers to touch him.

"No?" She flicked her tongue over his chest, a quick dart of pink feminine flesh before she looked up at him through long, dark lashes. "Just imagine how special you're going to feel by the time I wipe the smile off your face again tonight."

He appreciated a woman who knew what she wanted and how to get it. Yes, ma'am, he surely did. But her in-your-face bold promise reminded him that she'd angled to call the sexual shots last time, too. A point that made him curious as he unfastened her blouse and stripped her to a yellow satin bra.

Did she have to maintain control?

Maybe a better man wouldn't have tested the point. He had no doubt that she could deliver on her promise to wipe the smile from his face. Already she was doing a hell of a job of it as she lowered herself to her knees in front of him. No guy said no to this.

He could scarcely even think with her tongue sliding skillfully up and down his shaft, his cock growing painfully heavy as she guided him inside her small mouth.

It would be so easy to forget all about the power dynamics and just lose himself inside her—wherever she wanted him. But didn't he owe her better than that?

Didn't he want more than that from her?

Tough to recall when she gathered up her full breasts in her hands and pressed the soft swells on either side of an erection that throbbed so hard his eyes crossed. Every fiber of his being demanded he stop thinking and simply enjoy the moment. Except for one cursed freaking fiber, apparently. That vastly outnumbered part of him said he shouldn't waste the few chances this woman gave him by being as blind as the last man fortunate enough to touch her.

"Wait." With superhuman effort, he pulled himself away from the erotic thrill ride of her voluptuous breasts.

Dazed confusion and pleasure registered in her eyes as she peered up at him. Her lips were dark red and plump from her efforts, her breasts spilling out of the yellow bra to nudge his chest as he pulled her to her feet.

"What?" Her hands went back to the part of him that wanted her without question.

Definitely a woman who wanted to be in charge.

"I didn't get to taste you last time." He bent his head to her breast and drew on the stiff peak, needing to keep the sexual connection after she'd managed to fire him up so damn fast. "I'm going to address that oversight this time."

Her hands stilled on him for a moment, a fact that made it easier to think, to strategize, to remember all too vividly that it was better to give than receive when it came to sex. Well, actually either was damn good. But equally good.

He unfastened her bra and shifted his attention to her other breast, thinking maybe he'd imagined Donata's need for control. Inflamed by the scent of her, the heat of her skin, his hands drifted lower to help her shimmy out of her pants. They fell away in no time, leaving her standing in the middle of his living room in lemon yellow panties and giving him a serious thirst for lemonade.

But as he kissed his way south toward what he wanted, she seemed to shake herself out of sexual compliance. Stepping back, she tucked her thumbs into the waistband of her panties and stretched the elastic in a teasing display as she gyrated her hips to silent music.

"You want me to give you a private show?" Arching up on her toes, she spun around to present him with a view of her sweetly curved ass and the dimples just above each plump cheek.

She swayed her hips in a slow mimic of sex as she peered back over one shoulder.

He'd never had a lap dance before, but this was one female he'd gladly have invited onto his lap.

Damn, but she was good at making him forget what he was trying to do.

Too tempted by her dance to watch anymore, he wrapped her up in his arms, catching her from behind and holding her tight to his chest.

"Donata." He spoke softly into her ear, her blond curls tickling his cheek. "I'd never hurt you."

She stilled her seductive wriggle, tension stiffening her shoulders.

"I know that." She sounded sincere. Surprised, even. "I'd never be with you if I didn't trust you…physically."

Her qualifier spoke volumes about issues he wasn't ready to tackle. But if it was true, it raised more questions he *did* need to address.

No matter that having her spooned half-naked against him made him want to address other things.

"Then why do you have to be in charge? Why are you holding back?"

His hand found relatively safe terrain at her waist and he palmed the slight curve of her belly, stroking the soft skin while he waited.

"I don't know what you mean," she said finally, her voice slightly elevated in tone and a surefire indication she was lying.

"Come on, Donata." He kept her wrapped in his

arms, hoping he hadn't screwed himself over by asking questions she didn't want to face. "One of the things I admire most about you is that you speak your mind. Don't turn quiet on me now."

"I don't have to be in charge." She relaxed in his grasp a little bit, just enough so that he'd feel the difference, but not nearly enough to indicate she'd shrugged off deeper tensions.

"Honey, I hate to break this to you, but between the way you took control of things the last time we were together and your total discomfort with any role that involves receiving pleasure instead of doling it out, I'd say you're either hell-bent on being in charge or else...you like the power-trip factor of being a sexual dynamo."

He hadn't really considered the second scenario, but maybe she fit the profile as a woman who'd been taken advantage of sexually as a teenager.

Judging by her sudden rigid limbs in his arms, however, he didn't think she would agree.

"And just what the hell would you know?" She twisted around to look at him as she broke free of his hold. "I'm putting myself at risk enough just by messing around with a guy I'm working with. Why can't you enjoy what I'm ready to give instead of elbowing for more?"

She crossed her arms over her breasts and glared at him in the middle of his living room, communicating with her expression how much of a lowlife she considered him.

"I'm not asking you to give more." He reached out to skim a hand along her hips that remained too damn far away for his liking. "I'm asking you to relax. To forget about trying to impress me since you've already bowled me over. Just let me... touch you."

Gently, he drew her closer. Her feet inched forward at first, then he tugged harder until she landed chest to chest and hip to hip again.

"I wasn't trying to impress you." She rolled her eyes, but there was no heat in her words as he cupped her breasts in his palms.

"Give it up, Donata. You're crazy about me." He didn't know if it was true, but he thought maybe he could make her crazy about him, given half a chance.

The idea tantalized him. He'd been with plenty of women in the past few years, but none had intrigued him out of bed to the degree that Donata did.

"Don't flatter yourself." She kept her arms-folded stance, but she let herself be touched. Stroked. "Maybe I thought I owed you a little bedroom dazzle after the sexual harassment thing which was probably half the reason you left the force. You must have been an incredible cop."

He hadn't been expecting that—the guilt or the compliment.

"Thank you, but I wasn't a great cop." It had taken him a while to admit it to himself, but he could now that he'd found success in another direction.

"Bull—"

He fanned his fingers out over her breast and circled the tip, effectively cutting her off.

"It's true. Police work necessitates some ability to take direction and I've always sucked at that. When rumors of your accusations came to the fore, my captain gave me an ultimatum. Stop being such a loose cannon or turn in my badge."

He liked harassing her now just fine though. She was so soft under his hands.

"I made you lose your job."

"Hell no. You didn't even file a real complaint. If that was all I had against me, it would have been no big deal. But I was the precinct discipline problem because—as you so succinctly pointed out to me recently—I had that vigilante thing going." He'd hated the label, but there was some truth behind it. "Can you imagine how much a guy like me appreciated being given an ultimatum?"

A wicked grin curled around her lips.

"As much as you appreciate a woman playing the dominant role during sex?"

"I never said I couldn't handle giving over some sexual control." He dipped his finger into the waistband of her panties and then twisted the fabric around the digit to provide a little pressure where he wanted to touch her most. "I could barely stop drooling long enough to discuss the matter with you, as a matter of fact. But I think you deserve the whole gamut of offerings on the sexual smorgasbord."

She swayed lightly against him, brushing one breast and then the other across his bare chest.

"So you sacrificed for me?"

"Hell yes, I did." He stilled her teasing movements, more than ready to get this party started. "And to repay me for my efforts, I think you'd better quick get in touch with your inner docile vixen because I'm looking forward to taking the reins tonight."

DOCILE?

The man didn't know what he was asking and she had no intention of enlightening him since it would mean opening the cellar door to an assortment of personal demons she kept locked down there.

Breathing deep, she tried to relax into Sean's kiss and his amazingly buff bod pressed against hers. Not exactly a tough task since she definitely wanted him and the trick he did with rubbing her panties against her… She'd be putty in his hands in no time. But the particulars of this encounter could get scary.

Taking comfort from the feel of Sean's bicep beneath her questing fingers and the heat growing inside her, she reminded herself that she'd been turned on by the photo of herself wrapped in black leather bands from once upon a time, even though that had been the beginning of what she'd later recognized as an unhealthy trend. She'd liked playing captive to her man as much as the next woman, but Sergio's sexual tastes has gotten prohibitive when that kind of scenario became all he wanted.

She'd done docile to death, except she hadn't truly been submissive for most of it. She'd been seething with resentment that he hadn't let her play a role as a real partner in bed. She'd been a stand-in for his fantasy archetype—a woman who accepted that foreplay was a one-way street and that her pleasure should come from his pleasure.

Eeeew.

Worry had her wound tight as a spring even though Sean's mouth felt so good as he slid his tongue over her breast. She sensed she'd lose the battle of her worries soon, but then Sean arched back suddenly and looked at her.

Really looked at her. And oh, the man saw too much.

"Come with me." He spun on his heel and led her into a screened-off workout room complete with free weights, a TV and a treadmill along with a huge cache of outdoor recreational equipment. A bicycle hung from the rafters while skis, a snowboard and a golf bag rested against the far wall.

Her whole body tingled as they walked, her nerve endings pissed off at her for delaying Sean's touch.

"Um, Sean?" She'd never been much of an athlete, although she'd certainly put in her time with the weights at the police academy to build up her strength.

"We're just here for this." He looped his hand through a lanyard strap that rested on the handles of the treadmill and took down a stopwatch. "For you."

He held the watch out to her until she took the strap and studied the digital timepiece.

"Lovely. You're going to time our performance?" She'd never envisioned Sean as one of those guys who ran his life by a clock. He struck her as too much of a free spirit for that.

"Not exactly." He punched some buttons on the side of the stopwatch while she held the strap. "Well, sort of. Since you seem a little freaked out at the idea of giving over control, I thought maybe you'd appreciate knowing it was only temporary. Give me ten minutes to kiss you when and where I want, and then the show's over and you can do with me what you will."

He dangled the watch in front of her nose as if he could hypnotize her into doing what he wanted. Considering the way ten minutes sounded very manageable if it meant Sean would keep touching her, she figured maybe he knew exactly what he was doing.

"And I don't have to wear anything…costume-ish?" Flashbacks to nurse outfits and French maid getups made her shudder.

"Hell no. Wear what you want. Preferably nothing." He leaned closer to brush his cheek against hers and whisper in her ear. "So what do you think? Are you game to be all mine for a little while?"

The warmth of his breath on her neck sent a pleasurable shiver tripping over her skin.

"Count me in." She liked saying yes to this man, appreciated that he didn't take her compliance for granted.

He'd seen her fears and hadn't overanalyzed them. He just found a way around them. Her heart skipped with warm affection for him as he pressed the button on the stopwatch and released it to dangle from her arm.

And *oooh* my.

All at once, his touch seemed to be everywhere. His hands glided up her back to heat her skin, tunneling under her hair to graze her scalp and position her head to receive his kiss.

Hot, wet, possessive.

The angle he chose was dominating without being domineering and she closed her eyes to allow the feel of him, the feel of them together, to penetrate her mind.

And to her utter amazement, she realized she didn't feel like fighting this sensation at all. It was as if letting go—giving herself over to Sean—freed her. She didn't need to think about how to keep the upper hand since she knew she'd get it back in ten minutes. Her only thought was to enjoy this new-found freedom in relinquishing her pleasure to a man who truly wanted to make her feel good.

She clutched the strap of the stopwatch as he kissed her, touched her, walked her backward toward his bedroom. His thighs grazed hers, upping her awareness of him and what he wanted to do to her. Her legs burned wherever his thighs had brushed.

The restless anticipation in her veins assured her she wouldn't need the watch for the sake of telling time, but there was a certain joy in clutching the proof of Sean's caring, his sensitivity toward what she wanted.

Could there be a better indication of a man who cared about pleasuring a woman? His fingers smoothed over her hip to toy with her panty line and she thought she'd implode from the heat. The need.

But oh man, this guy didn't delude himself that pleasure originated in how skillfully he twisted his tongue, although—as he laid her back on his pillows and settled himself between her thighs—she acknowledged that skill was always lavishly appreciated. Ultimately, Sean respected that a woman's pleasure came from sources deeper than that, places inside her that were untouched by any physical caress.

The realizations swept over her as quickly as heat pooled in her womb. He swept her panties down her thighs, exposing her to the cool air of the room for only a moment before his breath warmed her there. Sean kissed her thighs and stroked her sex. He worked her clit with deft fingers, as he glanced up into her eyes.

Darkly sweet sensations built. Tensed. Tightened in the core of her as she waited breathlessly for release.

She couldn't look away from him. Her appreciation for what he'd given her couldn't be spoken aloud by someone as blunt as her because his gifts had been sweetly subtle and deeply personal.

Her eyes burned at the thought, but then he applied his mouth to her clit and she couldn't possibly think of anything but the intense build of lush pleasure.

So incredible. So intense.

Her thighs wrapped about his shoulders, her hips grinding against the unbearable sweetness of the act. She dug her fingernails into her palms to stretch out the feeling, wanting to hold on to this wild and mind-blowing moment. But then he pushed two fingers deep inside her as he kissed her and all was lost.

Lights exploded behind her eyes. Control flew out of her reach.

Her legs clamped tightly to him as her whole body arched in response to the pleasure knifing through her. Her cries bounced off the rafters to fill the room, her heart pumping so hard her blood pounded through her veins like an incoming tide.

Hard. Relentless.

Not until her cries subsided and her legs unclenched did she realize her stopwatch beeped with unrelenting insistence.

Apparently her time was up, but by now Donata was no longer sure she wanted it to be.

9

HE COULDN'T CONVINCE HER to spend the night.

Sean slumped into his seat at the computer long
after he'd walked her to her car, wondering what he
was doing in a relationship staggering beneath the
weight of old baggage. He didn't need Donata to
paint the full-color picture for him to know her one
and only past relationship had done major damage.
He respected that she'd ended up as wise and noble
hearted as she had, but beneath the layers of psycho-
logical crap her ex had given her, Sean wondered if
she'd ever work through those issues.

Then again, who said she had to? Wasn't it
enough that she was trying? And truth be told,
she'd done one hell of a job letting go of a few inhibitions tonight. He wouldn't think about this
night together without grinning for at least another
week. Sex with Donata had been phenomenal—so
amazing that he'd probably let go a few inhibitions
of his own. No matter that she hadn't taken him up
on his offer to spend the night, the truth was that
Sean hadn't ever extended a sleepover offer to a

woman since… How long had it been? He couldn't even remember.

He clicked through a few commands on the keyboard, making rounds that had become engrained in his routine since he'd made it his mission to protect exploited kids online. He still hated involving the cops in this case, even if one of the cops in question was a woman he was beginning to care about. And maybe that was another part of his concern with how things were escalating so fast with Donata. He was used to a lot of autonomy in all aspects of his life and he couldn't envision himself giving over control there either.

Good relationships were about compromise. He knew that in a peripheral sort of way from hearing one heartache story after the next while sitting on stakeouts. His work as a P.I. only underlined that knowledge since he fielded at least ten phone calls a week from people who were convinced a spouse or significant other was cheating and wanted proof.

Why did you need proof if you knew it in your gut already? Sean had learned from a client that the proof was a tool in the divorce or breakup. If proof was on your side, you didn't need to compromise because you won everything.

The whole conversation had made him nauseous.

And reminded him that *compromise* wasn't really in the vocabulary of a guy who'd been pursuing a case—hell, a whole crime trend—for four years straight.

Typing in a new URL, he accessed the video feed

from the bed-and-breakfast where he and Donata had set up a trap for whoever was interested in black-mailing her. The image was still there—the room empty and just the way they'd left it. With a few more taps on the keyboard he moved out of that image to double-check the link to Donata's old photo that he'd removed.

A sign he was in too deep already that he wanted to keep the Internet free of all private images of her? Hell yeah. He'd be thinking about her all night since the woman was becoming an obsession.

The list of names on the Web site's photo page still included Donata—something his tech guy hadn't messed with. But when he double-clicked her name, he was surprised when the pedophile self-help site didn't load right away. Yesterday the site had come up with lightning speed.

He checked the address bar and the routing code didn't look right either, although he hadn't written it down. This address had a ton of zeros in the code and the page remained blank as if a graphics-heavy image was loading.

Tension tightened his spine as he waited, know-ing this couldn't be good. If the Web site's techs had reloaded the photo image, it would have come over already since the page was stored in his computer's memory. This had to be something different, and— holy shit.

A live video stream image appeared on his screen. The color feed was excellent quality, complete with a clock loaded into the image to display real time. And right now, at 1:18 a.m. on the Upper East Side, Donata was unzipping her pants.

THANK GOD SHE kept her cell phone on.

Donata resisted the urge to wear a parka to the precinct to fill out a report. But she did indulge the desire to wrap herself in a chenille throw she kept on the back of her office chair for the days when the door to the street was opened too often. Now, as Mick finished taking her statement, it was all she could do not to bury her head under the blanket and lean on Sean, who sat in a chair beside her.

Thank God he'd seen the link. Thank God he'd called before she was naked. She'd started a litany of thanksgiving the moment she'd gotten his phone call early that morning and she hadn't let up the thankful prayers since she found a handful of tiny webcams around her home and not at the bed-and-breakfast where they'd tried to make someone fall into that trap.

Whoever had done this was easily staying one step ahead of them.

"And how long were you surfing the Web after Donata left your apartment last night, Sean?" Mick had leaned back from his computer, his haggard, handsome face showing every night he hadn't slept in the past week as he turned his attention to Sean.

"I was probably online for about twenty minutes before I found the video streaming images."

"But Donata said she'd been home for almost half an hour when you called her." Mick's gaze narrowed and she wondered what he was thinking.

"I picked up the loft a little before I sat down at the computer. I flipped the TV on and off maybe. I don't know."

"Did you call her as soon as you found the feed?"

"Jesus, Mick." Donata sat up straighter, unwilling to let her partner run down the person who'd saved her from exposing herself to the whole world.

Or, at least, a whole online community full of sexual deviants.

"It's okay." Sean didn't look pleased, but he glared at Mick with the same angry intensity Mick sent his way. "I'd ask the same thing. And yes, I called her apartment the second my brain processed what I was seeing. The first frame I saw said 1:18 a.m."

Donata couldn't help but remember that hadn't been long after they'd been naked together and she'd been vividly reminded how rewarding it could be to give up control now and then. She warmed just thinking about the way she'd forgotten the ten-minute time limit thanks to Sean's incredible means of distracting her.

"You have to admit, Beringer," Mick continued, "you spend a hell of a lot of time checking out Web sites that sell sexual images."

Sean's fist hit Donata's desk, scattering her pleasant remembrances of their time together.

"If you think I enjoy the sickening shit I have to see day after day in order to track these dirtballs after what happened to my sister—"

"Yeah. I figured. I know." Mick nodded. Closed his eyes. Looked like hell. "This case is pissing me off and it's got so many spirals and tangents I can't even feel like we're doing our job if we only take down a couple of these bastards. The more I investigate, the more I realize there's no end in sight."

Donata flipped the corner of the blanket against her chin, knowing things were getting worse at home for Mick instead of better. What would her life be like right now if she and Sergio had tied the knot and had kids? She'd be feuding with her kids' jailbird father through prison bars.

She shuddered.

"There's going to be an end. At least for the people who are planting the webcams and stealing video feeds. We still don't have much on the company packaging up the feeds as reality porn." No unsuspecting girls should end up with their bedroom adventures publicized this way. What if she and Sean had gone to her apartment tonight instead of his? Footage from their most private moments would already be in circulation.

"We could offer immunity to a couple of buyers for some help tracking the people behind fastgirlz." Mick sent the report he'd been working on and turned to look at Sean and Donata.

"No." Their answers were simultaneous.

Mick shook his head.

"That kind of attitude is exactly why Sean's been picking away at this case for so long. At some point you need to say enough is enough and make the arrests."

"But I'm not making any deals with the buyers of illegal porn to do it." Sean's jaw tightened as he spoke. "They need to face the consequences and have their habits unmasked in the community if we ever want to make a dent in the demand for this kind of product."

She tried not to bristle at his obvious attempt to run the show, but damn it, this had to be a decision made by the police. As much as she understood his anger at what happened to his sister, they couldn't allow a vendetta to dictate how they made arrests.

"I think whoever is tormenting me will show up at the bed-and-breakfast sooner or later." Donata intervened between the two men before tensions escalated. "I can stop by Sara Chapman's house on the way to the Hamptons tomorrow and talk to her again, maybe elicit something she wasn't ready to tell before."

"She also might feel more comfortable talking to a woman," Mick added, shoving away from his desk. "My daughter doesn't tell me anything either and she's about Sara's age."

"How is Katie doing?" Donata didn't want to pry, but she felt a small kinship with Mick's daughter and didn't want to see Katie land in the same sorts of trouble Donata had.

"Her mother has agreed to let her spend weekends

with me now that they're going to be in New York for the next year. Maybe it will help."

He didn't look too certain of that. Donata couldn't help but think his daughter was a lot more fortunate than some of the girls that had grown up on Donata's street.

"It will." She staggered to her feet, her eyes bleary from lack of sleep as she noticed the sun rising through a nearby window. "I'm going to book a hotel room nearby until my apartment is cleared and then I'll drive out to the Hamptons tomorrow afternoon. You want to ride over there together so you can keep up the search for the boyfriend?"

Mick shook his head as his cell phone went off. "I've got to pick up Katie at two, but I might head out that way earlier in the day. If you give me a call when you're ready to leave I'll try to meet you out there to at least present a united front to Sara's parents before I let you talk with Sara one-on-one."

Nodding, she tossed her blanket on the chair and picked up her purse, ready to finally end this day.

Mick's voice held her back.

"Donata, wait up." His cell was tucked against one shoulder and he waved her over. "It's the lab."

"They can't have results back already." She turned to see Sean shrug, weary lines etched around his eyes.

"Your partner is one of the department's best detectives and everybody likes the guy." He put a hand on the small of her back as they waited for news.

"Maybe the lab guys jump through hoops if he asks them to."

She didn't know how she felt about a system where some people got results faster than others, but she appreciated the way the department took crime against their own very seriously. For the first time at the 10th precinct, she felt important. She might not be a favorite among her colleagues, but she'd gotten the impression from everyone on duty tonight that targeting an officer—even her—pissed them off.

Mick clicked off his phone and tossed it on his desk.

"There were no prints at all on your computer or any of your own equipment, but we lucked out on the webcams. The lab found two sets of clear prints on both of them."

"You're kidding." Donata held herself very still, scarcely able to believe their luck. "This operation seems too smooth to leave evidence behind."

"Well, it's not great evidence since the only print they have on file belongs to Sergio Alteri."

The news hit her hard even with so many signs pointing in her ex's direction. She couldn't get her thoughts together enough to respond.

"I see." Sean's hand tightened around her waist. "Did the lab explain how a guy in federal prison can plant cameras in his old girlfriend's place?"

HER LIFE WAS UNRAVELING faster than she could patch it together.

As they sped east into Long Island late the next morning, Donata recognized the impending disintegration of the carefully constructed facades she'd placed all around herself in the wake of Hurricane Sergio. But she didn't have a clue how to build reinforcements at this point.

With each new day, another piece of her world chipped away in the maelstrom of a case that had become all too personal. The fact that she'd chosen now, of all times, to start sleeping with a guy who'd once arrested her only complicated matters.

"Are you going to be okay to talk to Sara Chapman today?" Sean's voice on the other side of the SUV scattered her worries for the moment as he reminded her about the upcoming conversation with the accidental porn star from the webcam tape. "You couldn't have gotten much sleep last night."

She'd let him drive today to smooth things over after a disagreement about where she should spend the night. She'd been exhausted after they left the police station at sunrise, and Sean had suggested she sleep at his house for a few hours to avoid the hassle of checking into a hotel. But she'd needed some space and hadn't budged on the hotel. Her wallet told her she was being obstinate, but her boundaries needed the regrouping time.

"I got a few hours." Fitful hours where she dreamed about Sergio coming after her to take revenge, his finger pointing in her face as he listed all the ways she'd sinned, all the reasons she'd never be a respectable, honorable person. Even in her dream she'd been pissed off that a man she despised could touch her self-esteem. "Enough to conduct a coherent interview but not quite enough to drive."

He didn't say anything else and Donata realized she'd need a hacksaw to cut the tension hovering between the leather bucket seats.

But had she done anything she needed to apologize for? So what if she hadn't felt right playing sleepover at his place? Wasn't a woman entitled to a few issues? This was hers, damn it.

Well, *one* of hers. There were possibly a few others rattling around her subconscious if she cared to think it. Which she didn't.

The silence stretched, broken only by some inane deejay on a local radio station.

She debated discussing the interview strategy with him, but ultimately figured she'd do better relying on feminine instinct when she spoke to Sara.

Then the radio snapped off and Sean released a gusty sigh.

"I put a call in to Ray Brook this morning. The prison where they're holding Sergio."

Everything inside her stilled. Quieted. Froze.

"What?" She'd heard wrong. There was no other explanation for him trampling her territory in this case without her permission.

"I wanted to find out how hard it would be to get in to see him if it comes down to that. But as it turns out, you're on his approved visitor list."

Her skin turned cold and sweaty at the same time, a sick clamminess that made her want to crawl back in bed. Or indulge the tide of pissed-off anger headed Sean's way. She knew that Sergio had added her name to his visitor list—giving her an open invitation to see him while he was locked up—so it's not like she was surprised to hear it. But what business did Sean have to take the initiative where Sergio was concerned?

"I didn't say much about you taking down the link to my photo even though I asked you to wait in case we needed it for evidence."

"But you didn't need it—"

"That's not the point and I think you know it. I've been a detective for exactly two months, Sean, and I don't appreciate you steering this investigation for me just because you've got more experience. The fact is, it's my badge on the line this time and I don't want to give it up simply because you're determined to play rogue agent and call the shots."

"I knew you'd want to talk to him eventually." He kept his voice cool, reasonable.

Unlike hers, which drifted higher as her frustration wound tighter.

"You *don't* know that. The man would gladly skewer me for turning evidence against him. I'm sure the only reason he added my name to his list was in the vain hope he could strangle me if I came to see him." She gasped for deeper breaths, hoping the added oxygen would cool the clammy heat creeping all over her. "And even if I do want to talk to him down the road, I'd prefer to make the arrangements myself when the time is right because I sure as hell am not going to put myself in a position where the department is giving *me* an ultimatum to leave."

She must have driven the point home because Sean went utterly silent on the other side of the SUV, leaving her with anger rapidly cooling into a fear she couldn't take back her words.

MICK WAS WAITING in the driveway of the Chapman house when they arrived and Sean welcomed Donata's partner's presence to defray the tension pulled taut during the trip to Massapequa.

Sean hung back as Mick and Donata went to the door, remaining outside to check out the Chapmans' little slice of suburbia. They lived in a modest house with a basketball hoop in the driveway and a big-ass barbecue grill on a side patio. It was the kind of lifestyle Sean had walked away from more than once since the idea of settling down had seemed so final. So…staid.

Did Donata want this kind of life one day? Most women he had dated in the past did. The ones with bigger budgets dreamed the same dreams, but on a different scale. To them, the suburbs meant Connecticut and the gas grill was a little more high tech. It all added up to the same thing in Sean's mind.

Too isolated from real life to keep him entertained. Too content with the status quo when he pictured himself more as a mover and shaker.

But then, Donata's voice entered his brain as he stared up at the Chapman house and he could almost hear her argue that he just wanted to play *rogue agent* whatever the hell that meant to her.

So, okay, maybe he knew what that meant. Why couldn't she understand that he liked getting results without having to play the games involved with police department politics or kissing his captain's ass to get the assignments he wanted?

Maybe he was used to getting his own way. Wasn't there something to be said for having enough self-awareness to understand how you worked best? Looking at it from that perspective, he'd made a great decision by leaving the police force.

And—applying it to his personal life—he'd made a great decision to remain resolutely single. No wife, no kids, no shacking up just for the hell of it. Guys who didn't like to follow anyone else's rules were better off that way. Donata's explosion on the drive over here had been a much-needed wake-up call.

Too bad nothing sucked quite like a ringing alarm in the middle of a good dream.

He stood watching a furniture truck delivering a couch to the house next door, wondering how much longer Donata would be before they drove the rest of the way to Southampton. When a movement out of the corner of one eye caught his attention, he whipped his head around to see a kid—a scrawny, dark-haired boy in his late teens—spin on the rubber sole of one sneaker in the middle of the Chapmans' rose garden.

And didn't that seem a little suspicious?

Sean took off after him just to see who the kid might be. A cop might blow off stuff like chasing teenagers through back fences and across three properties since most guys on the force didn't want to risk the scandals and scathing rumors that came with hauling in the wrong people. Picking up his pace, Sean just leaped a few garbage cans and ducked a clothesline that held a couple of frozen sheets before he collared the kid.

"What's your hurry?" He pulled the teen backward by his sweatshirt, more than a little curious what the kid had to hide.

"You're a cop." Still trying to scramble away, the boy spit at Sean's shoes, making it abundantly clear what he thought of law enforcement. Sean tugged him back into the Chapmans' yard.

"Actually, you're wrong there." Sean adjusted his hold to bring the kid up short, lifting him off his feet so they were eye level. "I'm not a cop, so I don't need to worry about your rights or your well-being if I decide I want to talk. Who the hell are you?"

The kid looked ready to spit again when Mick and Donata came charging through the back door of the house, followed by five people he could only assume made up the Chapman family.

Mick's gun was trained on the kid while the older woman behind Donata pointed toward them.

"That's him! That's Sara's ex-boyfriend." Her dark glare convicted the kid as she reached for her teenage daughter as if to protect her from further harm. "He's the one who bought her the webcams and hooked them up for her. Why don't you ask him how my baby's pictures ended up plastered all over the Internet?"

Donata, meanwhile, stalked closer. Her eyes were fixed on the pale, sweaty kid Sean held. And, oddly, the would-be escapee seemed as interested in her, judging by the way he swallowed hard as he watched her.

Almost as if…they knew one another?

"T.J. Malone." She withdrew her badge from her jacket pocket and flashed it under the boy's nose. "I sure hope you have a good reason for being here."

10

As Sean dropped the kid on his feet, Donata stared into the eyes of one of Sergio's many godsons and wondered how a good kid could screw up his life this badly. The last time she'd seen T.J., he'd been a straight-A student who shown up at Serg's house every now and again to help out with computer trouble. Serg had been a complete washout with technology and he liked to brag that T.J., son of a friend who worked at his auto body shop, knew more about computers than anyone on the garage's pay-roll.

Probably an overstatement, but Sergio had always been skilled at drawing people in and making them feel appreciated. An excellent talent for a man whose success depended on the aid of people who were slavishly devoted to him.

She pulled her coat tighter around her shoulders and waited for T.J. to say something, his surly street expression at odds with the signs of suburban life all around them. A rusty chain on a nearby swing set squeaked as it blew in the wind.

"Maybe T.J. would remember his reason for being here if he came into the station with me," Mick offered.

Donata hadn't realized he'd followed her across the Chapmans' backyard while the family waited on the deck. Mick looked at her strangely for a moment before his gaze darted to Sean, making Donata realize she'd inadvertently stood inches from Sean when she came on the scene, well within his personal space. When had her body become so in synch with his that she moved toward him automatically?

"It's Terrance now," T.J. corrected him, his angry attitude something new for him as he straightened his clothes. He turned to Donata. "And I dropped the Malone when my dad walked out. I don't want to be identified with any guy too much of a chicken shit to raise his own kids."

She remembered Sergio saying something about the kid's father having an affair. Apparently T.J.— Terrance Joseph—had taken it hard. No wonder she hadn't recognized Sara's boyfriend's name on the reports Mick had filed during his other interviews. She'd never heard of Terrance Russell. Maybe he'd started using his mother's maiden name.

"So you have no respect for your own father, but you thought it would be a good idea to take direction from a man in federal prison?" Donata studied him carefully since body language often accounted for the most valuable information given when questioning a suspect.

She didn't have to look at Sean beside her to

know he was doing the same thing right now—watching and gauging the kid's reactions. Would they be able to compare notes on this new turn later, or had she pissed him off too much to continue working closely with him?

The thought churned uncomfortably inside her, worries coming faster than the wind whipping her hair past her ears.

"I don't know what you're talking about." Terrance scowled back and forth between Sean and Donata. "I thought you said you weren't a cop?"

Donata glanced over to Sean, wondering how that topic had come up and how much Sean had said to the teen.

"I'm not." Sean glowered unpleasantly. "They kicked me out for being too rough with suspects. Just ask her."

Clearly he was trying to intimidate the kid. An unwise tactic when they needed his cooperation since there was no way he could be behind the larger crime of illegal film distribution.

She was about to intervene when the boy paled.

"I didn't hurt anybody." He twisted unsuccessfully against Sean's hold. "Sara wanted to make the tape. We were going to split the cash and use it to get out of here after she graduates. Then she got mad at me when her parents found out about the video and she faked like she didn't know the thing was going to be a moneymaker for us."

Donata wondered how much of this conversation

the family could hear as they stood watching from some thirty yards away. Five other lawns backed up to the same property and Donata noticed plenty of blinds shifting on nearby windows to take in the suburban drama.

"This was going to be your moneymaker?" Sean's voice growled into the cold wind, animal-like and angry. "She's an underage girl, you dumb ass. You could go to jail for statutory rape alone, let alone all the other ways you've taken advantage of her. And you think your father's a bad guy for walking out on his family? Take a look in the mirror, kid, because you're turning out a hell of a lot worse than the old man. At least he tried to suck it up and make his family work."

Donata didn't know who was more surprised by the outburst, her or Terrance. She agreed with Sean, but she didn't know what good it would do to yell at the kid and scare off any hope they had of getting him to cooperate.

Thankfully, Mick stepped between Sean and T.J., taking the kid's arm.

"I think we need to have a long talk." He took his handcuffs out and clicked them open. "I'll let you decide if you want to have a group discussion inside the Chapman home or if you'd rather head down to the police station and make a formal statement. Either way, you might end up under arrest at the end of the day. What'll it be, kid?"

Donata saw Terrance relax a little, his shoulders

sagging even as his face remained unnaturally pale. Maybe having Mick and Sean play good cop/bad cop wasn't such a bad thing.

"I'll talk here." His eyes cut to Sean. "As long as he's not there."

Sean backed up a step.

"Works for me. That animosity you're feeling for me goes both ways, believe me."

He turned and walked toward the driveway and Donata realized how hard it had to be for him to talk calmly to someone like Terrance who had engaged in crimes similar to those his sister's boyfriend had committed. Sean knew how devastating a *money-maker* video could be when deviants of all kinds got hold of the footage. How could kids sell out one another that way? Especially when they claimed to love the person they were filming?

On the way into the house, Donata hung back to ring Sean's cell phone to let him know she'd rent a car to take to the Hamptons later. There was no point in having him wait around for her to finish when this could take hours.

Her call went straight to voice mail. A sign he wasn't picking up calls from her?

She left her message and followed Mick inside, wondering if maybe a little of the animosity Sean felt toward Terrance, toward criminals in general and even toward the NYPD, would one day extend to her, too.

Maybe, she admitted, it already had.

SEAN CHECKED INTO the Southampton bed-and-breakfast under an assumed name thanks to the wide choice of ID he had to back up a variety of covers. He was damn good at the technology aspects of his work, even if some people thought he pushed too hard in other areas of his field.

Donata, for one. And didn't it suck to be turned on by a woman who pissed him off so much? He couldn't stick around her questioning of Terrance when the kid-glove method of handling the little creep made him insane.

But then, Donata wasn't the only one who thought he pushed too hard. His former precinct chief had taken the same stance. Even his own sister, who'd moved to Montana three years ago and since married.

She'd told Sean just last week that she didn't appreciate him making a lifelong vendetta out of an incident she'd put behind her years ago. It had become a sore spot for them, a topic they normally agreed to leave alone. Except last week Sean had heard rumors that the Chapman family was taking the tape of their daughter to the police and he'd been upset that his hard work might be undone by a bunch of well-meaning cops who would only look at the smaller picture.

As Sean unpacked his clothes for at least one overnight at the bed-and-breakfast, he kept an eye on the parking lot below for signs of Donata's arrival. He'd arrived in town a few hours earlier after receiving her message, figuring he would use the time to check out her old stomping grounds from her days with Sergio.

The couple had summered in the Hamptons, but their main house had been in the city. When he'd arrested Donata, he'd picked her up at the Manhattan house, so he'd never seen their lifestyle in Southampton.

Closing the curtain to the parking lot below, Sean couldn't deny the wealth of resentment at her words to him earlier that day. She'd basically accused him of being asked to leave the force when that hadn't been the truth. He was given an ultimatum, damn it, not asked to leave.

And she'd had a hand in putting him in that position with her noisy accusations. Had she forgotten that part of the equation?

At least back then, he'd been able to admire her in-your-face style that called attention to itself even while she surprised him with how competent she was.

These days, Sean saw more and more of that quiet competence, less of the brash-talking firebrand. Had she changed that much? And which one was real?

He'd just set up his computer to check the feed from her hotel room when a knock sounded on his door.

"Who is it?" Standing, he rechecked the scene in the parking lot below.

No help, really, since he didn't know what kind of car Donata would have rented to make the trip.

"It's me." A soft feminine voice drifted through the door. "May I come in?"

Adrenaline shot through him in automatic response. Jesus, two nights together and he was turning into Pavlov's dog, drooling on cue at the sound of this woman's voice.

"Depends." He wanted her in his room in spite of the way she'd gutted him earlier. That didn't mean he couldn't give her a hard time about it first. "Are you willing to concede you stretched the truth when you said the department asked me to leave?"

"Depends. Are you willing to admit you make a lot of executive decisions when we're supposed to be working together?"

He leaned against the door, willing to wait.

"I asked you first."

There was a long pause.

"I had no right to fling your past in your face and I'm sorry." Her lowered voice came through the door in a rush of words. "Your way of doing business makes me nervous. And I'm a little wary of men who don't take my position into account so I may have stooped to slinging a low blow."

It took him a minute to unlock the door as he tried to process all that she'd packed in to her statement. When he did unbolt the lock, he found her in the hallway with her purse, her overnight bag at her feet and her jacket still on, spotted with a few damp places from the light snow falling outside.

Wisps of her wavy blond hair sprang out of a dark

scarf she had wrapped around her head, her cheeks red from the cold and wind. Her dark, double-breasted jacket was buttoned hip to neck, but not even the heavy lined wool could disguise her generous breasts.

"I take your position into account. Why haven't you dropped off your bags yet?" He looked around the empty hall, watchful and wary.

Whoever rigged the camera on her apartment computer could be following her and while Sean knew her police training would help her handle the situation, he'd rather not be caught unaware.

"I wanted to find out if you've checked the web-cam we planted to make sure no one is watching." She bent to retrieve her overnight bag and he had to ease her out of the way to take it from her.

Bad enough she thought he took advantage of her to do whatever the hell he wanted to with regard to her case. Did she have to think he was totally unchivalrous too?

Men couldn't win with women today.

"I haven't checked the feed yet. I was just about to do that when you knocked." He settled her bag on the floor near a small love seat and gestured for her to have a seat. "You want a drink? I stopped off on the way here to get some bottled water, some orange juice and a few beers."

She flopped down into the love seat, unbuttoning her coat.

"Am I on duty? I don't even know anymore. I've

worked so many days straight since we took on the Chapman case. If I'm not on the clock, I'll take the beer."

He grabbed two since his mouth was going dry watching her unbutton the fastenings on her coat. Didn't matter how many layers a woman wore. Watching her take any of them off was sexy.

"You're working too hard." He clicked the keys on his computer to bring up the surveillance feed from her room at the bed-and-breakfast, then he headed over to the love seat to give her the drink.

The temptation to slide into the seat next to her was strong, but he forced himself to maintain a little distance and paced the room instead. Being near her stirred up his senses.

"But I can feel we're getting closer." She shimmied out of the coat and took a long swig straight from the bottle. "The talk with T.J.—Terrance—wasn't terribly helpful, but at least he admitted to selling the footage. He uploaded it to a link on the fastgirlz Web site that has since vanished, and apparently he signed a release giving the company permission to reproduce it. He says Sara signed it too, but he admitted she might not have realized at the time what it was for. Mick took him down to a local station to make a statement."

He watched her hair play peekaboo with a tiny scar on her neck he hadn't noticed before. The need to kiss that hidden patch of pale skin was driving him crazy.

"The kid had to know Sara couldn't legally sign

away rights she doesn't have as a minor." It made him angry to think how willingly the girl had participated in her own exploitation.

"He said he thought it was just a formality and that no one at the film company would really look twice at the document." She shrugged out of her suit jacket next, revealing a pale blue satin-and-lace camisole that had barely shown under her conservative suit.

Sean took another drink of his beer and tried not to make his slow perusal of her neck and shoulders, her breasts and narrow waist, too obvious. The whole suite conspired against him with the romantic frou-frou of complimentary champagne and two red roses beside the bed.

"Was the kid smart enough to keep a copy of the release form?"

"Yes. He's got it, and Sara's parents weren't too happy to hear it. They've already contacted their lawyer and are talking about a civil suit if they can't pin anything on the boy criminally. I think he'll at least do time for a statutory rape charge."

"But you don't think this kid is the one who planted the webcam in your apartment? He's got a strong tie to Sergio so he'd have access to your old photos and he's got a vested interest in making Alteri happy."

"He's got an alibi at the auto body shop, apparently. We'll double-check it, but I wouldn't think he'd be apt to come all the way into the city to plant a webcam on an old broad like me when there's a much better market for tender young flesh like Sara's."

"Some of us are far more turned on by women who are legal. And for the record, you're way hotter now than you were in those centerfold pictures."

She smiled and shook her head.

"Is that the Michelob talking?"

"I'm serious. Besides, you can't forget that whoever planted those webcams in your apartment is probably more interested in blackmail than anything, so Sergio's godson makes a strong candidate. Is Mick going to take his prints?"

Whoever the bastard was that trespassed in Donata's house to plant that equipment, Sean wanted him behind bars. Which reminded him he needed to check the feed on her room to make sure no one had tried the same trick here.

"He'll take prints, but I'm not holding my breath. I think my blackmailer is tied into the filmmaking industry a lot more deeply than someone like T.J."

She strode over to where he sat at the computer and watched him rewind through the footage from the past few hours. The soft floral scent of her triggered immediate sensory memories of tasting her skin, the warmth of his breath intensifying that fragrance.

The monotonous screen on the computer showed no changes in her room, no disturbance by any intruder, giving Sean no visual distraction from the thrill ride of his memories.

They were so hot together. So combustible. He wondered how long they could be in the same room alone together before the heat flamed out of control.

And yet…shouldn't he hold even a little residual anger toward her? Yes, she'd apologized for the low blow of saying he'd been asked to leave the department. But there had been something else that should have put him on guard….

Oh yeah.

"When you first came in here tonight, you said you were wary of men who didn't take your position into account." She'd slid it neatly into her apology, so it had sort of snuck up on him. He planned to address it before things went any further tonight. "I have to say I don't appreciate being compared to your gangster ex."

She turned on her heel and walked away from him, taking her scent and her bombshell body with her.

"You and my ex fight on the opposite sides of the law, so I can see where you wouldn't appreciate the similarities. But you're both powerful men who are used to running the show. I don't want to be maneuvered and managed ever again. It's part of the reason I don't give up control well, even though you've proven that handing over the reins can be extremely rewarding in bed." The siren's smile she sent his way nearly undid him then and there. "But I'd prefer that the bedroom was the only place where I had to make that decision."

WAS IT SO HARD to give her that much?

Donata studied Sean as he seemed to weigh his options and her wishes. He had to know that she was putting herself on the line here to even talk about how they related to one another since that implied...a relationship? She wasn't totally comfortable with the idea herself, but they couldn't keep going on the way they were, working together with remote professionalism during the day, then heating up the sheets together at night, only to repeat the cycle the next day. Their day and nighttime worlds were bound to collide sooner or later.

He pushed out of his seat to come closer, making it more difficult to think objectively as he stalked across the lushly decorated Victorian suite. Fabric spilled on the floor from the generous sweep of curtains and even the dressing table legs were skirted with yards of white damask. Pillows erupted from the bed in all sizes and shapes, obvious invitations to linger...

Wasn't it strange how the impending approach of a man she was attracted to could make her so fully aware of her own body when he hadn't even touched her yet? It seemed a scientific impossibility for her skin to anticipate his touch and yet she swore that's what happened as he closed the space between them. Her satin-and-lace camisole left her bare shoulders particularly vulnerable to the phantom touches.

"I have strong opinions." He stopped inches away from her, staring down at her from his taller height. "I happen to think I'm right a lot of the time, so I can't just stop acting on those opinions."

Her mind raced ahead to refute his words even if the rest of her body wouldn't back her up. Her knees already wobbled with the need to fall into his arms. Into him.

"No one gets their way all the time."

"That's why you're more than welcome to argue with me, tell me I'm wrong, and act according to your own opinions. But I'm going to be honest and tell you that compromise isn't always an option for me."

She couldn't hold back a surprised laugh. How arrogant was that?

"You're kidding."

"I'm not. That's why I took the out from the NYPD. I had to put myself in a position where I could succeed despite myself." One side of his mouth lifted in a half-hearted smile.

She would *not* let herself be charmed by a man who'd just admitted he didn't bend for anyone. Maybe it was the scent of the roses on the nightstand that was making her feel decidedly charmed anyway. She found herself thinking about what it would be like to find retreat in that pillow-filled bed and drink champagne from Sean's mouth all night long. With an effort, she fought to combat his incendiary words.

"I can see where your approach might work in your professional world, but I'm curious to know if anyone you've ever dated has bought into this personality quirk." She didn't mean to pry, but she'd shared so much about her past while she didn't know anything about Sean's.

His hazel eyes shifted to a darker brown, his half smile fading.

"Isn't asking each other about past relationships off limits?"

She'd hit a nerve. But didn't she deserve to know something about him beyond the compelling, attractive man she saw with her own eyes? Experience had taught her that a person's past provides their deepest passions, their most intriguing peculiarities of character.

"For a man who refuses to compromise, I would think a woman would have to be a little more pushy than normal."

"Then maybe we're perfect together."

Now it was her turn to smile.

"Why do I have the feeling I've just been insulted?"

He reached for her and she found it impossible to walk away from the touch she'd been thinking about all day. His fingers skimmed her shoulders, the backs of her arms. She fought the urge to close her eyes and sink all the more deeply into the sensations he could create for her with only his hands.

His voice lowered as he came closer, the masculine tone vibrating along her nerve endings.

"I don't know, but I meant it in the nicest possible way."

11

SHE MADE HIM think too much.

Sean knew the questions she raised would rattle around his head all night, especially later when she would refuse to sleep in his bed. But then again, the incredible thing about Donata was that she also knew when it was better not to think about anything at all.

Like now.

His hands trailed down her rib cage to her waist, molding the narrow curves before ascending to her breasts, lifting them in his hands. She arched onto her toes in response, sighing into him with her whole body.

And just like that he went from turned-on to sexually intense. Something about her sparked a sense of possessiveness he'd never had with any other woman, a need to cover her, take her, make her his own.

Not questioning the instinct, he simply followed it. He pulled the silky camisole over her head, unveiling her breasts encased in sheer blue mesh with narrow strips of satin covering dark pink nipples.

"So beautiful," he muttered to himself as much as to her, awed all over again how so much blatant femininity lurked beneath the cover of her forceful personality.

He bent to kiss the soft fullness spilling over one mesh cup when she bracketed his face in her hands.

"That first night we were together and you let me be in charge each time…that was a kind of compromise, right?"

Something shifted inside him to think she would try and see the best in him.

"You're damn right that was compromise because I wanted to call all the shots very badly. Bottom line, however, I wanted you with me more."

Her smile was so full, so unreserved, she damn near knocked him out with the dazzle of it.

"What about now?" She played with her bra strap, flicking the nylon on and off one shoulder while she waited for his reply.

"I want you all over me right now." He gripped her hips to his for emphasis.

Hell, if he was honest, he gripped her hips just for the pleasure of it.

"Then why don't you let me savor just one tiny compromise?"

He knew whatever it was would probably torment him beyond reason, but then he only had himself to blame.

"Yes, but I might need to ask for the time limit tonight." If she wanted to put off the inevitable, he'd appreciate knowing that eventually he could have her completely at his mercy.

"Fair enough." She stroked her hand over his fly. "I get to taste you tonight, but only for a reasonable length of time."

His erection strained the seams at the thought of her lips wrapped around him, that perfect Cupid's bow leaving a bright red lipstick print on his shaft. Yeah, he could definitely agree to this. Besides, he had an idea how he could stave off completion. It wouldn't be easy, but it would be fun trying.

SHE SHOULDN'T BE so attracted to a man this sure of himself, this unyielding, this unwilling to meet her halfway.

But oh my God, she was attracted.

Her knees wobbled with want as she unfastened the buttons of Sean's shirt and undid his belt. Her progress was slowed by his hands foraging into her bra, into her panties, anywhere she let him before she remembered her mission.

Her whole body tingled by the time she succeeded in undressing him, and she realized that her clothes were gone too, all except for the blue mesh thong that scarcely covered anything anyhow.

She also realized with some surprise that they had ended up in the bedroom of his small suite situated right next door to hers. She didn't need a bed for what she wanted to do with him, but she didn't mind when he drew her into the turned-down sheets on top of him.

Knees between his legs, she twirled her tongue around the tip of him, savoring the hot silkiness of his skin in contrast to the rock-hard feel of his erection. She wrapped her hand around the base of him, steadying him for slow entry into her mouth.

Delicious. She shivered in response to his low growl of response and she savored the knowledge that she could elicit an animal response from him. The imitation of the sex act sent a pulse of hunger between her legs, her thong damp with need. He touched her there and she whimpered in response, her knees moving to straddle his leg for better access.

The world receded to nothing but steam heat and sensation, her mouth working over him in slick repetition as he touched her and teased her and broke the fragile string of her panties so that he might touch all of her.

The room was pitch-dark, sensations narrowed to touches and tastes, her tongue stroking him as he slowly turned her whole body around. Her mouth never left him as he parted her thighs to taste her, too.

Exquisite pleasure pierced her along with his tongue, the slick heat of his mouth on her too much to bear. An orgasm ripped through her in one harsh spasm after another, her senses flying apart in a thousand pieces as light flashed before her eyes. She slumped to one side of him on the bed and she thought perhaps she fainted for a moment because the next thing she knew, Sean had already sheathed himself in a condom and was straddling her body still shaking with little aftershocks.

And then he pushed his way inside her and all the

pleasure before then felt like nothing compared to the hard heat of him between her thighs. She tilted her hips to accommodate him, gladly accepting every inch of him inside her.

He stretched her hands over her head, pinning them there in a subtle message of domination that would have freaked her out a week ago. Now, she gave herself up to him gladly, delighting in the way they could switch who had the upper hand at different times.

This was what sex should be like.

And, for those couples who cared enough to try, she knew that in a committed relationship, that was what love would be like. Not that she had any intention of finding out while her past still haunted her all too literally.

But as she reached her second climax just before Sean shouted his release, she couldn't help but dream.

SEAN COULDN'T STIFLE the small sense of triumph he experienced at seeing Donata fall asleep in his arms.

In his bed.

Would she be aggravated with herself—with him—when she awoke to realize how easily she'd drifted into slumber beside him with the scent of roses and champagne in the air? Maybe. But perhaps tonight would force her to see she was swimming against the tide by trying to deny the inevitable. They might not see eye-to-eye and they might piss each other off on a regular basis, but bottom line they couldn't keep their hands off each other. There was something deeply compelling about the chemistry between them and he didn't see any point in fighting it until it ran its course.

What happened after that...he didn't want to go there. Not now, while her hair spilled over his arm in a silky wave, her soft exhalations warming his shoulder as she turned toward him in her sleep. She looked so sweetly peaceful with her lashes fanned out across her cheeks. And young. One tended to forget her youth when she was awake and barreling through life with guns drawn.

He smoothed a lock of hair that had fallen across her cheek, stroking it back into position with the rest. He was just bending down to kiss her when he heard a noise on the other side of the floral-covered wall.

A small thump.

He stilled, knowing the room on that side of his suite belonged to Donata. The bed-and-breakfast was an antiquated Victorian with sprawling wings and strangely shaped rooms, so perhaps there could be a crawl space between them.

Instinct told him otherwise.

Easing out of bed, he slid into his jeans and buttoned them on the way to the sitting area where his computer rested on a coffee table. He'd been re-winding through the webcam feed on one screen, so he opened a new window to view the feed live.

Nothing.

Not one to ignore his instincts despite what technology said, he grabbed his gun and the room key Donata had laid near her purse earlier. Stealing out into the hallway, he took two steps before running into a young woman coming around the corner, her arms laden with a heavy silver tray and a steaming teapot. She gave a start upon seeing him—or maybe she was just startled to see the gun—and Sean had to steady the tray to keep it from spilling.

"Sorry," he offered automatically, grinning amiably to offset the surprise. "I heard something in my friend's room next door and I knew she was in here with me." He gestured toward his suite while the woman in her late teens or early twenties—the innkeeper's daughter, maybe?—blatantly stared at his bare chest.

He flexed his pecs for good measure as he reestablished the tray in her arms.

"Oh yes. I see." She blushed and nodded awkwardly, clearly flustered. "My mother said Ms. Casale had been working late and thought she might like some tea before bed."

"That's very nice. I'll bet she'd like that." He took the tray back and wondered if it had really been his pecs that had caused the nervous blushing or if she might be hiding something.

"Okay. Thank you." She backed up a step, her running shoes quiet on the thick area rugs that covered the hardwood floors.

"Did you hear anything inside Ms. Casale's room just now?"

"Me?" She shook her head, her long dark ponytail swishing in denial. "I didn't hear anything."

The young woman bounded down the stairs before he could ask her anything else, and he stalked back to his suite with the tray in one hand, weapon in the other.

"Is everything okay?" Donata's voice greeted him as she swung open the door, her eyes wide, her service revolver in her hand. She wore his dress shirt but hadn't bothered to find a pair of pants so her long legs were exposed from midthigh.

"Everything is better than okay." He let his gaze linger on her legs. "I was just out slaving over a hot stove for you."

"Um, thank you." She set down her gun and followed him into the sitting area where two floral chintz love seats sat facing one another with his laptop on the table in between. "Although the last I checked, making tea didn't require much slaving over a stove. Especially when the water has been heated and hand-delivered by a cute girl."

"Busted." He watched her pour a cup for herself, the steam wafting up around her face in a thin tendril.

"My room is undisturbed?"

"I'll check the feed again, but I think it's all clear. I just heard something on the other side of the wall and when I went out there, I spotted her with a tray."

"But?" She peered at him quizzically, as if she'd guessed there was more to the story.

"But I thought I heard a noise from inside the

room and I'm not sure why the maid—or whoever she was—seemed so nervous."

"A strange, half-naked man surprised her in the hallway with a drawn gun? I can tell you why she was so nervous." She sipped her tea on the love seat beside him as he reviewed the last half hour of the feed. "Why? Do you think someone could have paid her to plant a webcam?"

"It pays to be suspicious, as you know well."

"Could anyone ever rig the feed on those cameras of yours?" Donata passed him the cup of tea in offering.

Sean stilled.

Holy shit.

He flew off the small couch, half knocking over his laptop as he reached for her room key and bolted out the door.

THE WHOLE SETUP HAD been tampered with. New webcams had been installed on the laptop Donata had left as bait and now fed a bogus loop that showed the room completely undisturbed. In addition, the hidden computer and webcams they'd placed in the closet to keep watch over the room had been redirected with the same misinformation technology.

"Whoever this bastard is, he's damn good with this equipment." Sean's movements were brittle as he hauled the small computer out of the closet wearing latex gloves so as not to stir fingerprints they both knew wouldn't be there.

Still, they weren't taking any more chances with whoever was tracking Donata.

"But everything is disconnected now?" The idea of hidden cameras watching her every move made her twitchy and nervous.

"Everything's down." His clipped words told her he blamed himself. "Our feed looked clean because whoever broke into the room reprogrammed the video stream to continually play the same image of the empty room instead of actually recording what was going on. I should have been suspicious when I scanned though the footage earlier and never saw a maid come in. I should have known it'd been sabotaged."

"You couldn't have known." She'd already touched base with Mick and discovered Terrance Russell's fingerprints didn't match the one they'd found on the other computer equipment found in her Manhattan apartment.

Their leads were turning up one dead end after another. They were holding T.J. on suspicion on a variety of sexual misdemeanors until they could convince his ex-girlfriend, Sara, to come in and make a statement.

"I could have called in for more tech support on this case, and that's what I'm doing next because I don't think like the geek squad." He had his hidden computer stripped down to bare essentials and seem to be firing off e-mails as he spoke.

Sending out an SOS to his computer guy?

At least he had a plan. Donata didn't have a clue how to catch the phantom stalker, the video-obsessed watcher who lurked in the shadows of her life, unless she did what she'd been dreading for days. And that option scared her spitless.

Mick hadn't come up with any better ideas, telling her they should touch base later while they thought about their next move, but Donata couldn't decide if he was distracted by his own problems, or if he was playing mentor to her by prodding her to figure out the next step on her own.

Scratch that. Mick was too good of a cop to let his home life interfere with their case. So that meant he was just waiting for Donata to admit there was only one other logical path she should be following.

"So we're going to admit defeat and wait for someone else to follow an electronic trail?" What happened to the days when a good cop smoked out the bad guys on wits and cunning?

God she wished she could put off the inevitable.

"Do you have a better suggestion?" The black look Sean gave her wasn't exactly encouraging.

"As a matter of fact, I do." Damn it. Damn it. Damn it. "I think the time has come that we pay a visit to an old friend of mine."

His scowl faded as one eyebrow rose. Clearly, he'd been as content as her to delay this particular meeting.

"Jesus, Donata." He let out a gusty breath. "Are you sure you want to do that?"

No.

She didn't want to do that. But she'd do her job no matter what the personal costs might be.

"If my past has a connection to the illegal videos, I think it's worth facing a few old ghosts to put an end to it once and for all."

12

RAY BROOK FEDERAL Correction Institution was about a six-hour drive from the city. Sean and Mick had both volunteered to make the trip with her, but she knew Mick had been enduring the week from hell with his daughter sneaking around and his ex-wife threatening to take Katie back to Europe.

As for Sean… She'd declined his company because she wasn't sure she wanted any witnesses if she fell apart after seeing Sergio. Not that she had any warm-hearted feelings left for the man who'd lied to her more ways than she could count. She just worried that seeing him would chink away—okay, sledgehammer away—at the self-esteem she'd busted her hump to build. And she'd rather Sean continue to see her through the lens of her police work than as the poor sap teenager who'd let a gangster play savior for her.

Therefore, she'd navigated her way through the Adirondack Mountains on her own, sliding off the road once on a hairy turn in Lake Placid and then winding her way over Route 86 to Ray Brook, a medium security lockup for male offenders.

Now, as she stood unmoving for the metal detector hand wand as part of visitor in-processing, Donata told herself she wasn't immature enough to rejoice over the depressingly austere setting of her ex's current home despite the idyllic mountain setting outside the gray walls. Still, she couldn't deny feeling relieved to see how securely locked away he'd been for the last four years.

Not that she'd ever thought doing time in a federal pen was a picnic, but every now and then she saw those shows on TV suggesting wealthy criminals could buy their way into cushy facilities. If that was true in some cases, it sure as hell hadn't happened for Sergio Alteri, judging by the stern expressions of the prison guards outside the visiting room.

She would have received a slightly warmer reception if she'd admitted to being a cop, but since this wasn't an official inquiry, she hadn't wanted to wait around for court approval to see him. Besides, Sergio would definitely snub her completely if she showed up in an official capacity. This way—taking him up on his long-ago offer for a visit—she might be able to learn something useful. Of course, first she'd have to listen to him rant and whine about all the ways she'd screwed him over by turning evidence against him. That was the only reason he'd added her to his visitor list after arriving here. But maybe after that she would be able to find out who had access to his old photographs or who he might have entrusted to make her life hell.

She stood behind a woman with a baby in one arm and a toddler in the other as she waited in line to have her hand imprinted with a black-light stamp, the last step in the process to enter the visiting room. Donata wondered how the lady in front of her managed raising two kids with her significant other in jail. As it was, the overwhelmed mama could barely convince the guards to let her bring baby supplies into the visiting area, since apparently the number of diapers allowed was regulated.

Finally, she was admitted to the room that looked sort of like a high school cafeteria. Institutional tables were scattered around an open space with two guards to oversee the visitors. There were no telephones and bulletproof glass the way they liked to show in the movies. Just a small assortment of visitors and inmates in white T-shirts, trousers, belts and prison issue shoes.

None of the prisoners were Sergio, but then she'd read that the visitors were usually escorted into the room before the inmate they wanted to see. Donata chose a table in the corner, far away from the other groups scattered around the room, and waited.

A minute later, Sergio strutted in.

He didn't see her at first, his gaze sweeping the room. She noted he wasn't as big as she remembered. Prison food had made him thinner, his skin hanging a little looser on his tall frame.

But then, he probably seemed bigger in her dreams because—good or bad—he'd been an integral part of her life and he loomed large on the horizon of her memories. His hair was neatly combed, short and dark with more gray at the temples than she remembered. He had to be nearing fifty. He wasn't wearing his glasses today, but then he didn't actually need them. The wire-rimmed lenses she remembered had been more for show and they had worked like a charm on her as a teenager. She'd looked up into his bespectacled face and pegged him as a smart guy. A reader.

Only later did she find out he'd never even read a whole newspaper, let alone a book.

He spotted her then and his placid expression changed. She'd been expecting anger and resentment but she could swear he looked almost pleased as he strolled past a couple of families toward her table.

"Hey, babe. You couldn't stay away, could you?" He swooped down to kiss her on the mouth under the guards' watchful eyes.

The kiss was too quick and unexpected to shove him away. Not that she really could have since starting a fight with Sergio might mean she'd be asked to leave.

He looked quite satisfied with himself as he folded his tall body into the bench alongside the table, taking up too much room near her.

"I had to get the kiss in right away since the guards only go for physical contact at the start and at the end of a visit. Even then, you have to be careful not to open your mouth or they'll bust it up. Lots of drugs get passed along with the tongue, you know." He folded his hands on the table like a model prisoner and looked her up and down. "I figured my need to kiss a woman—any woman—outweighs the fact that you're a cop *and* the bitch who turned me in."

Smiling, he stared openly at her breasts and waited for her to speak.

Lucky for him she needed his cooperation today or she'd show him how much of a bitch she'd like to be. His words didn't begin to touch her since she'd long ago learned that a bitch was just a Babe In Total Control of Herself. Some men didn't appreciate women like that.

"Who told you I'm a cop?" She kept her voice down and was grateful he had, too. "You still keep in contact with your old friends?"

He shrugged. "Going to prison lets a guy know who his real friends are. The people who keep in touch have my back. The others who don't reply to my letters for months on end…" He moved his gaze up from her chest long enough to glare at her. "They don't mean anything to me anymore."

In a different environment, she would have been relieved to know she never crossed this man's mind. But right now, she had a game to play if she wanted to find out anything.

Pouting like a woman who knows how to get her own way, she told herself she could be an actress for half an hour if it meant closing a case.

"What about your chick on the side? You remember, the one you screwed ten ways to Sunday until I decided to screw you in return? Does she still write to you?" Until that moment, Donata hadn't really considered her old rival as a possible suspect since illegal porn was more often a man's crime. But now that she thought about it, she supposed Rosario Gillespie had every reason to hate her.

"Rosie?" Sergio smiled, probably enjoying the thought that he'd cheated on the woman who helped send him to prison. "Her old man is too much of a hard-ass to let her write to me after he found out about us. Last I heard, he moved Rosie to the sticks to keep her out of trouble."

He turned to watch a fight break out between the mother of two and her inmate husband, an argument quickly halted by prison guards who removed the man from the visiting room and escorted the crying woman and her two kids out the other door. Poor kids.

"How do you know?" she prompted, remembering how difficult it could be to keep Serg on track. She'd always suspected he had ADHD. "Who's writing to you if not dear sweet Rosie?"

"Don't *dear sweet Rosie* me when you propositioned my own nephew."

"Only because he was suspected of shady things." She'd hated that part of her informant gig. The FBI had directed her movements with a heavy hand and while she didn't owe Serg any great loyalty, she'd never liked the idea of cozying up to the nephew.

Thank God Alec Messina had been a much more upstanding guy than his uncle.

Serg snorted, disbelieving.

"Seriously, Sergio, who's taking care of things back home while you're in here? I noticed the Southampton property looks like hell." She focused narrowly on the conversation to help tune out the smell of sweat and institutional food.

"No shit?" He straightened, predictably image-conscious.

"By Southampton standards anyway. You don't have one of your boys swinging by now and then to check on it?" She studied her nails like the answer didn't matter, amazed how easily she could lapse into old conversational patterns since it wouldn't be the first time she'd had to work him around to get answers.

The task hadn't been too difficult since Serg wasn't the sharpest tack, but the old trick made her realize how much she wanted a relationship where honesty and forthright discussion won out over manipulation.

"Big Joey goes over there sometimes. He's supposed to contract with the lawn guys and keep the place rented until I get back."

"You cleaned out the Southampton house?"

"We're renting it furnished. Joey put all my other stuff in storage."

Giving the guy free access to old photos of Donata? She still couldn't imagine why Big Joey would want to target her personally, unless he ran the illegal porn ring and only used the photos for blackmail purposes when she took the case.

Still, that didn't explain why the photos had been given to some crappy online site for free viewing.

"What about the New York house? I know the feds seized it, but did you get to move your things out first?"

"Are you kidding? They took everything that wasn't nailed down for evidence. You want to tell me how my big-screen TV was evidence?"

"What about your computer?" She knew his prints had been on the equipment installed on her PC. "Where did that go?"

"How would I know?" He smacked his hand on the table, drawing the attention of a guard across the room. "Why don't you ask your friends the feds? They probably planted evidence on it before they confiscated it."

The visit pretty much deteriorated from there with Donata asking leading questions that went nowhere and Sergio growing more and more belligerent.

Finally, convinced she wouldn't find out anything else by being nice, Donata switched tactics.

"Look, Serg, I did you a favor today by coming to see you without the benefit of my law enforcement status." She kept her voice low, knowing that inmates were apt to make life hell for any of their own they suspected of cooperating with the police.

"It's true then?" He grinned like a kid with a secret. "Can I call you next time I get stopped for speeding?"

She knew he was kidding, but for a moment, she remembered what it had been like when they first met, before he'd taken up the family business of crime. She'd never be attracted to him again, but she could remember what had charmed her as a teenager. His lame jokes and his willingness to be the guy who told goofy jokes had given her the false sense of security that he was a simple man. A safe man.

"Depends. Did you give one of your guys access to naked pictures of me?" She cut to the chase and studied his expression. She might not be an expert judge of people, but she'd lived with this man long enough to have learned when he was lying.

"Naked?" He adjusted his trousers. "Jesus, Donata. I'm doing a fifteen-year bid here and they sure as hell don't allow conjugal visits. Don't talk to me about naked anything."

"This is important or, believe me, I wouldn't be asking. Someone's circulating photos that only you would have access to. If it's not you, I need to know who would have those pictures."

He remained silent for a long moment, his face unreadable. Hard. She wondered if prison had changed him.

"What'll you do for me if I give you some ideas?"

Irritation flared along with the urge to show Sergio how much she'd learned in her physical training for this job. She'd love to kick his butt.

"Either you know or you don't know. I'm not doing jack shit for you since you earned your trip here. As far as I'm concerned, if you can't help me out now, I'll be only too glad to see what else we can convict your sorry ass for to stretch that fifteen years out as long as possible." She hadn't ever really gotten the chance to lash out at him since she'd had to play a role as his girlfriend to be an informant.

It felt good to speak her mind now, even if it meant her visit to Ray Brook proved a bust.

"You've changed." A hint of admiration lit his eyes.

"Thank God for small favors."

He shook his head, shoulders slumping with weariness.

"I don't know who would take those pictures. Hell, I don't even remember where they were if I wanted to see them myself." His eyes cruised slowly over her and she had the distinct impression he was recreating the scene in his mind.

"So you don't know who's blackmailing me."

"Blackmail?" His shoulders perked up along with his expression.

"Someone doesn't want me to bust an illegal porn ring and they're using a blast from the past in the form of those stupid pictures to keep me quiet."

"You?" Sergio rolled his eyes. "Good luck to those guys, eh? Although I wouldn't mind a copy of that photo of you if you happen to have it handy. A man needs entertainment behind bars. The movies suck here."

She waited, unwilling to be drawn into more inane conversation about his need for diversion, but slightly pleased that at least she'd left Sergio with a lasting impression that she wasn't a woman to mess with.

"I don't know about any illegal porn rings, but then, when I was on the outside, I was never the kind of guy to want a picture over the real thing." He scratched his head and leaned back on the bench. "But if I had to guess who might go through my stuff when I'm not around, I'd say the list is pretty long. Besides Big Joey, who am I going to trust?"

"And no one's asked you or Joey about access to your stuff recently?"

"Wait." He frowned. "Joe did tell me one of his friends wanted a list of some… Well, shit, I can't tell a cop what he wanted."

"I'm not interested in some two-bit drug deal. Whoever is blackmailing me is taking pictures of half-naked little girls and passing it off as porn."

The frown deepened, furrowing deep lines around his mouth. Thankfully, there was still a small amount of honor among criminals. Even if Sergio had taken her home with him when she was sixteen, she'd kept her age a secret for the first year because he truly wasn't the kind of guy who would have hit on a kid.

"Bastards. The guy's name was Ford. Richie Ford." He eased back to peer around the visiting room, perhaps to make sure no one had overheard the conversation. "That must be worth a few bucks to you, right?"

"It might be, but then I happen to know you're

richer than Midas even after the feds took the Manhattan assets. So why don't you just consider this your first act of kindness on your path to rehabilitation, okay?" She stood, grateful this chapter in her life was over and oddly relieved that her ex hadn't been the one blackmailing her. She hadn't realized how much she hoped the guy wasn't behind an illegal porn operation until she took her first deep breath in a week.

Bad enough she'd lived with a gangster extortionist who'd threatened the life of an FBI agent. But if she'd lived with a man who took footage of unsuspecting teenagers…

Shudder.

"You're gonna mention my generosity to the parole board, right?" He smoothed his shirt front and smoothed back his hair. The gesture reminded her what he'd said about only getting to kiss visitors at the beginning and end of a visit.

"If the tip is good, I'll let them know." She kept her voice low, maintaining her original intent not to let any of the other inmates know Sergio had been visiting with a cop.

Now, she hurried away just as he was reaching for her since she wanted nothing to do with another kiss. She had so much more with Sean now than she'd ever shared with Sergio.

"In your dreams, Serg." She waved at him instead of letting him kiss her.

"Come back anytime," he called as a guard stepped

forward to escort him back to his cell. "Weekends are good for me."

She had to smile. Not that she found anything humorous about Sergio's jail time. No, she felt the smile come from deeper inside her after a visit that left her feeling a little less guilt-ridden about her past and more than ready to meet her future squarely. The stigma of a gangster boyfriend didn't have to dog her forever.

The feeling of freedom amazed her and scared her at the same time since she realized she had no excuses to hold back with Sean any longer. At least, no excuses by way of her past. And that's where the fear came in. She had a hot tip that could bring her case to a close and could end her time with Sean along with it.

The thought stung more than she would have guessed.

She didn't know if her future would be one that Sean would want any part of, but for this one moment, she took a lot of satisfaction from knowing she'd done the best she could in her life considering the circumstances of her early years.

But before she could go out and discover what the future might hold, she had a pressing engagement with Richie Ford.

13

AFTER SITTING in a briefing meeting the next afternoon with Donata, Mick and the chief of their detective division, Sean was ready to have Donata all to himself.

As he drove her back to her apartment for the first time since the webcams had been discovered, he realized that he should be grateful the police department had acknowledged his expertise on this particular case and let him listen in on the briefing. But his mind wasn't on work after spending the whole previous day worrying about Donata.

His fears weren't logical. Physically, she'd be safe enough at a prison and she knew how to take care of herself. But what would it do to her heart and her head to sit in a visitor's room across from the creep who'd put her through hell?

Sean hated the guy with a fierceness that surprised him since he knew all the rage was on Donata's behalf.

"So you went over the technical details in the briefing," he said aloud as he parked the car across the street from her place. "But what kind of vibe did you get from the guy? Is he still angry with you for turning on him?"

He wouldn't have liked the idea of her going to any federal pen by herself, but visiting this one in particular had bugged him since he knew she was vulnerable to her ex even if she didn't care about him anymore.

"He wasn't as resentful as I feared, but then almost four years is a long time to get over it." She stepped into the street before he could get her door and they walked into her building together.

"So it wasn't too awkward?"

She slowed her pace as they approached the elevator. Her building was small, with no doorman and no security beyond a callbox for residents to buzz in their visitors.

"Of course it was awkward. Just picture going to see one of your exes in prison. You've got all the angst of a relationship gone sour plus the cold hard reality to face that your romantic judgment was so bad you not only picked a loser, you picked a criminal."

Grateful the elevator arrived on that note, Sean held the door for Donata.

"None of my exes would have wanted to see me since I'm the king of short term." He pressed the button for her floor and shoved his hands in his pockets. He was glad to have her back, but this wasn't the way he pictured a reunion with the woman he'd thought about nonstop in her absence.

"Is that a hint?" She cocked her head sideways, as if the straight-on view of him didn't make any sense so she needed to adjust her angle.

"A hint about what?" The elevator doors swished opened and he waited for her to exit.

"A hint to me not to expect too much from whatever it is that's going on between us. A hint that you won't be sticking around for long." She reached for the button to hold the door open, her gaze never leaving his face.

"Hell no. I just meant to say that despite the disappointment of having someone you care about turn out to be a bad guy, at least you know you meant something to your ex. The man still wanted to see you in jail, even knowing you turned him in. Obviously this guy was crazy about you."

"Or just plain crazy." She emerged onto her floor finally, her eyes sweeping the hall in typical cop fashion.

He waited while she unlocked her door, glad to have escaped that conversational thread.

"So why would you crown yourself king of short term if you can admire a long relationship even when one of the parties has a rap sheet?" She let him in, tossing her keys on the coffee table and dropping her bag beside them.

And he thought he'd escaped this conversation?

Fat chance.

Donata sounded as though she was only warming up as she made her way around the apartment, throwing off her winter coat and booting up her computer.

They'd come here under the pretext of researching Richie Ford, but it wouldn't be the first time one of their work nights had taken a turn for the personal.

"Honestly?" Sean shrugged. "I don't think much about my personal life to have an opinion one way or the other. Ever since my sister was hurt, I've been a little obsessed with work. Not just because I wanted to clean up some of the danger spots online, but because I started my own business."

She gestured toward the computer desk where her new laptop rested since her old one remained in the police evidence room. He accepted her unspoken gesture and took the seat, wondering when they'd developed wordless communication.

"Your business certainly looks successful enough where you could afford to lighten up the workload by now." She disappeared into her bathroom and he knew she would be changing her clothes.

Another moment of intimate knowledge that he understood about her. She liked to shed her work clothes for something softer when she came home.

But then, visions of Donata stripping off her clothes in the other room weren't going to solve their case any time soon so he forced his fingers to start clicking keys.

"Word of mouth has been great," he admitted, proud of how quickly his business had developed. "Especially for a private investigations business. Normally, people think you're barely scraping by if you're a P.I., just working for peanuts to make your next rent check. Plus there's a preconceived notion that you'll take any kind of seedy job that comes your way."

She reemerged wearing the low-slung jeans she favored and he found himself wondering if he'd get a glimpse of that hummingbird tattoo that hovered on her lower back. The jeans had red flowers embroidered down the length of one leg and a silk scarf with similar flowers—a kind of wild roses?—in the print woven through the belt loops. A white T-shirt tucked into the worn denim, the fabric void of decoration save for one red heart stamped in the middle.

"Really?" She ran a hand through her hair as if to loosen it, her fingers half scratching her scalp as she kicked up the curls. "Since when do you care what people think about you?"

"I don't care what anyone thinks of me on a personal basis, but I'm definitely invested in the perception of my business."

Grinning, she strutted past him to pull two sodas out of her refrigerator and he found himself holding his breath waiting for that flash of skin at her waist as her T-shirt rode up with each swaggering step. If he didn't get to work soon, he'd have those long legs of hers wrapped around his waist in no time and she deserved more than a quickie in the middle of an investigation.

Besides, she might have her ex on her mind after her visit to the prison and Sean needed to be one hundred and twenty percent sure she was over the guy before he plunged himself heart-deep inside her again.

"So you left the department to be a rebel, but

you founded a business that forces you to play conservative."

He took a deep breath—not that it helped much—and opted to lose himself in work rather than in her luscious body.

"That's about the size of it." He forced himself to do a couple of basic searches on their new suspect, running multiple windows at once to see what he could find. "You live and learn. But for someone like me, it's easier to take direction from myself than to have some desk-bound lieutenant telling me what to do."

She nodded as she set down his drink on a butterfly coaster next to the computer.

"Sometimes success is just a matter of knowing your strengths and finding ways to work around your weaknesses. Obviously, you're doing a great job on both counts." She took a long drink as she went back to stare into her pantry while he continued to work. "But we got terribly off topic from why you're the king of short term, didn't we?"

"Isn't that a good thing?" His fingers stalled on the keyboard. "I never mind talking about work."

She peered over the low cupboard door at him as if he'd said something revealing. He went back to his search.

"Maybe relationships will turn out like your work," she observed finally, as she seemed to be chopping something up on a cutting board.

Did he really want to know what that meant?

Damn it. He did.

"How so?" He pushed back from the computer to hear her better.

"In the world, you just needed to find the right job where you could be yourself and not feel like someone else was bossing you around." She'd already chopped up some cheese. Now she was slicing a baguette to throw in a basket alongside the platter.

"Right." He got up and peeked in her fridge and found some cold cuts to add to the platter that was strictly chick food to his eyes.

"So maybe you've been doing the short-term thing because you haven't found the right woman who lets you be yourself and doesn't try to manipulate you."

Her words might not have resonated with him if he hadn't been trying to sneak ham slices onto her platter. As it was, the moment seemed rich with "aha" meaning as she carried the silver tray—ham and all—over to the coffee table.

"Would you bring the bread basket?" she called over one shoulder.

"Got it." He picked up the bread and told himself that people didn't fall in love over cold cuts.

But for the first time, he could visualize a future for himself that involved more than work. He'd never been able to imagine being comfortable enough with a woman to want to face the inevitable challenges of a future together. But with someone like Donata, someone who threw herself into work the same way he did, who was as passionate as him, he could see himself kissing the short-term title goodbye.

AFTER HOURS of investigative work, Donata wanted to bang her head on the nearest wall. Sean swore the case was coming together, but there were too many pieces that didn't fit neatly, too much crime on all sides of this illegal webcam racket.

They'd at least made some progress on Richie Ford. He was so clean that they'd already determined he must have an alias or two if he was a friend of Serg's. Sure enough, they'd found another name he'd done business under was also a name once listed as a contact for fastgirlz. The name had been a dead end when Sean had first investigated the company, but now some of the leads from the past were beginning to make sense.

Richie Ford, aka Richie Feyette, was definitely up to illegal activities. But Donata wasn't sure why he had a beef with her personally or how he was getting illegal videos made all over the city. Surely he couldn't sneak into that many bedrooms by himself.

Even with all the ways the case was finally starting to fall into place, Donata found herself distracted by Sean's shoulders as he worked at the keyboard, his back straight and muscular. Sometimes she dipped her head closer to his shoulder just so she could find his scent and breathe it in.

She told herself she wouldn't have allowed herself to be distracted if her utmost attention would lead to a faster arrest. But she wouldn't be able to question Richie until the morning at the earliest. Besides, she'd spent serious overtime on the case all week, including the trip to Ray Brook and one sleepless night at the precinct after her apartment had been compromised.

Didn't she deserve to make a move on a man who might be out of her life as soon as they started making the arrests that would close the Sara Chapman case?

"This is our guy." Sean turned toward her suddenly, his eyes bright with passion for the job more than passion for her. "He's involved in a slew of Web sites advertising illegal movies and I just got word from the online superstore that his *fstgrlz* e-mail address is behind hundreds of webcam gifts through their wish list feature. That's not how Sara Chapman received her webcam, but if we contact a few other gift recipients we should be able to strengthen our case against him."

She blinked at the barrage of information when she'd been thinking along far more carnal lines.

"We still need to tie him to Sara Chapman if I'm going to close her case." Her brain operated at the speed of sludge, but she forced herself to consider her options. "Our only real link so far is that both Terrance Russell and Richie Ford are friends of Serg's. They could be working together."

She didn't like the idea of T.J. falling so far from grace that he'd date girls just to obtain illicit video footage to sell at a profit.

"Maybe you could talk to Terrance again. Bring up Richie's name and see what happens." He threaded his fingers in her hair, tilting her face up to his. "Are you okay?"

Better now. His touch sent a shot of sexual adrenaline through her tired body.

"Yeah. Just a little brain-dead after reevaluating our information so many times."

His hand slid away from her as he glanced at the face of his watch, a massive silver timepiece with multiple readouts and buttons. She'd be lucky to locate a clock on there at all.

"It's after midnight. No wonder you're tired." He reached for his coat before she could make it clear she wasn't too tired to jump him, just too tired to think.

Her cell phone trilled obnoxiously, halting her from reaching for him.

The caller ID showed an unfamiliar number.

"Casale." It wasn't easy summoning up her work voice when she was exhausted and sex-starved, but she did her best.

"Donata?" A young woman's voice was on the other end, her tone unsure and maybe nervous.

"Yes, this is Donata. Who's calling?" She motioned to Sean to wait.

"It's Katie Juarez. I'm sorry to call so late."

Mick's daughter? A knot twisted in her gut.

"Hi, Katie. Is your dad okay?" Her tiredness dissolved in a moment of panic. Nothing could happen to him…what would she do?

"He's fine. But he's going to be really angry with

me if he finds out what I did." Her voice broke on the other end of the call.

Donata's fears for Mick doubled since the only thing worse than something happening to him would be something happening to his kid and she had the feeling Katie was in trouble.

Late-night phone calls from scared teenagers were never a good sign. She reached for Sean, grateful for his warm strength as she squeezed his arm.

"Where are you? Are you hurt?"

"I'm on Long Beach. At a friend's house." The girl sniffled. "I'm okay here. But I did something really stupid after Dad went off on me two days ago about being irresponsible."

Donata couldn't imagine how Katie got her cell number unless Mick had given it to her for an emergency. Something struck Donata as strange about the whole conversation since she hardly knew Katie.

"My dad told me about the case you've been working on and he started quizzing me about my computer use and tracking every stupid Web site I've ever visited. It was really invasive, you know?" The girl's voice contained a hint of foreignness, but then she'd been raised abroad until last fall.

"I'm sure he just wanted to keep you safe. What did you do?" Donata found it a little challenging to empathize with a girl whose father cared so deeply about her and wanted to be involved in her life when Donata's dad had been quick to push

Donata out into the real world to find her happiness as an individual.

Translation—on her own. By herself. Alone.

"My boyfriend had been asking me to make him a present for his birthday, but I'd been telling him no because I didn't feel comfortable."

Oh damn. Damn. Damn.

"What did he want you to do, Katie?" Donata sat on the sofa since her legs had grown weak. Sean disappeared into the kitchen and reemerged with a glass of water for her.

Had she ever sounded as young as the girl on the other end of the phone? This naive? Donata knew she had, but the thought of being that vulnerable made her heart ache for Katie.

"He wanted a few…photos." She spoke softly, as if she didn't want someone to overhear her. "Not a whole video like in that case my dad said you guys are working on. It was just a picture or two that he wanted to snap with his camera phone."

Donata's heart plummeted.

"So you let your boyfriend take the pictures because you were mad at your father?" She didn't mean to sound judgmental to a girl already on a guilt trip, but Donata needed to get the facts straight in case any of this tied into their investigation.

"Not exactly. I took the pictures myself because we haven't even done anything yet. He hadn't ever seen me naked before."

Donata couldn't help but think that nakedness

was better shared in person for a girl's first time, but at the same time, she felt relieved that at least Katie's relationship hadn't escalated.

At twenty-seven, Donata wasn't even sure *she* felt emotionally equipped to deal with intimacy. How the hell could a teenager?

"And you've already sent him the pictures?"

Tears started in earnest then, or so it sounded from the broken sobs.

"I just hit the Send button about half an hour ago. But instead of feeling empowered the way I imagined I would, I just feel like crap."

Donata didn't know how she could fix this for Mick's daughter who obviously had a good head on her shoulders despite this unwise move. But she did know she needed to talk to this young woman face to face to share a little hard-won wisdom before she got herself into any more trouble.

"Katie? I need to see you as soon as possible. Tonight." She drank the water Sean had brought her, grateful for the look of concern in his eyes. When had a man ever been worried about her going out in the middle of the night alone? Serg might have been jealous, but never worried for her safety.

Jotting down the address, Donata knew she'd just found a way to finally make peace with her past. Maybe all the mistakes would be made more worthwhile if they helped prevent someone else from making them, too.

14

"WHAT DO YOU MEAN, it's a setup?" Donata stared at him across the console of his SUV, not bothering to hide her exasperation with him and their case spiraling out of control.

Sean had let her drive his vehicle since he wanted to check out a few things about Katie's story on the way and he couldn't if he was behind the wheel. They were driving toward a Long Beach address in next to no traffic so navigating the road was easy enough. Navigating the mood inside the SUV was anything but.

They were both tense and frustrated. Lack of sex the past two days didn't help. At least not on his end. Working next to her all evening without touching her had been painful.

"Don't you think it's strange that she called you for help and advice even though she's only met you a couple of times?" He'd checked a reverse address directory to find out who owned the property Katie claimed to be staying at, but he'd only come up with a corporation name that didn't match the friend's name Katie gave. Of course, the property could be rented.

"At first I thought it was strange, but if she's feuding with her parents she obviously didn't want to share her misdeed with them if she could help it. And she knew about this case because Mick talked to her about online dangers, so it makes sense that she'd think I could help with a similar situation." She moved into the right lane to exit while Sean worked through the scenario in his head.

"I can't believe Mick didn't want to meet us out here." If it had been his kid, he would have called in the SWAT team to get her out and bring her home. Or to a convent.

"He said he didn't want to upset her since his hard-nosed tactics apparently drove her to rebel in the first place. He's letting me talk to her, but he'll be at his ex-wife's house when we bring her home later so the three of them can have a sit-down."

"But he didn't even know this so-called friend of hers."

"Apparently she receives considerable freedom from her mother, so Mick doesn't make the calls about where she spends her time."

Sean wondered what she thought about that since she'd been vocal about her father's lack of involvement in her own life. Maybe both Donata and her partner had a little too much personal connection to this case to see it objectively because Sean's every instinct screamed at him that something didn't feel right tonight.

And wasn't that an eye opener?

He'd been squeezed out of the NYPD for too much personal connection to a case after his sister had been molested and he hadn't been able to see how much that compromised his work. Now, four years later as he watched Donata and Mick make decisions that didn't necessarily employ their best professional judgment, he finally recognized how right his department had been to come down hard on him for running rogue on his sister's case.

And if it took him four years to face the facts, what were the chances Donata would understand she might be too close to this case in the next few minutes?

The houses were tightly packed in this section of Long Beach, with one balcony on top of another as they neared the water.

"I'm not letting you go in alone."

"And just who do you think is going to be inside that house besides a freaked-out girl, her friend and possibly a pilfered beer?" Donata lifted her directions to study them under the dashboard light as they sat at an intersection.

"I don't know. Maybe a jacked-up boyfriend who works for fastgirlz and doesn't want his gravy train to stop so he takes out the cop who threatens it?"

She paused long enough to at least consider the idea.

"Mick went all through his daughter's computer. Don't you think if anything came up that could be a potential red flag he would have been all over it? I think it's safe to assume she hasn't been receiving suspicious e-mails or visiting questionable Web sites."

Donata turned right up a connector road through the middle of Long Beach. Trinket shops and fast-food places sat side by side with upscale restaurants and small boutiques.

As they passed an Italian place with a deep red awning and soft candlelight glowing through the windows in the dining room, it occurred to Sean that he'd never even taken Donata on a real date. What kind of a schmuck wooed a woman by sleeping with her at every opportunity and failing to give her anything vaguely resembling romance?

"But she had a relationship with this boyfriend who wanted naked pictures and no trail of that was on her computer. Who's to say she doesn't have other friends that don't show up on her hard drive?"

Maybe she was buying his point because she pursed her lips in thought. He liked that she listened to him, that she validated his ideas by not brushing them off the way the top brass had when he was a detective. She might not play as fast and loose with an investigation as he would, but she wasn't so strait-laced she couldn't see someone else's perspective either.

"Plus you said this is her first year going to school in New York. That kind of transition is bound to make a kid feel isolated at best and make her a target for these kinds of operations at worst."

Donata blinked fast and gave a jerky nod.

"The kids most at risk are the ones who don't have a good support system at home."

Sean reached out to her across the console, rubbing her shoulders with whatever assurance his touch could offer. He assumed she was thinking about her own past since it had to upset a strong woman like Donata to think she'd once been somebody's target. So it surprised him when she whispered, "This is going to kill Mick."

Sean ignored the pang of jealousy to hear her speak another guy's name with that kind of tenderness. They were just friends. And being partners forged a strong bond in a hurry. Logically, he knew that.

But damn, he wanted to hear her say his name with that breathy softness that meant she cared.

"It should be just up ahead here on the right." He pointed to a house number a few digits higher than the one they were looking for.

Donata cut the lights and pulled over. Sean closed his laptop and shoved it in the case under the passenger seat.

"So what do you say we call some backup just to be safe?" He'd definitely made headway with her on the way over. He had to at least make the suggestion.

But she was shaking her head before the words were even all the way out of his mouth.

"And risk advertising Katie's misstep to the whole world with a big showdown in residential Long Beach? I don't think so." She eyed him in the shadowy interior of the SUV lit only by a streetlight two houses up. "You can back me up better than a rookie with a patrol car. How about we go to the door together, but once we see inside the house to make sure everything is kosher, you wait outside?"

It was more of a compromise than he would have been able to make if his sister had been involved. And while Sean would feel better with a small army of protection where Donata was concerned, he appreciated her trust in him to do the job as well as any of her colleagues.

"Good enough." He watched her check the safety on her weapon as quickly as she checked her lipstick in the mirror. Seeing the two acts in quick succession spoke to the strange nature of this encounter since they weren't sure if they were greeting an enemy or coming to the rescue for a friend's daughter tonight.

He damned well hoped it was the latter because he knew what he was like when the people closest to him were threatened. And if an enemy waited on the other side of the door to this crappy three-story walk-up, they were about to find out that messing with Donata had been a very big mistake.

THE HOUSE SEEMED LEGIT, Donata thought after talking to Katie for almost an hour. It hadn't really been the home of a friend, the way she'd said on the phone. Instead, her boyfriend's brother rented the place as a summer hangout with friends, but the apartment was vacant half the year.

Definitely not a safe place for a fifteen-year-old girl to sleep over, but it fit with her story and didn't seem like a setup to lure Donata out. As much as Donata was sick and tired of dead ends in the case, she'd be grateful if this turned out to be one since she didn't want Katie mixed up in any of the crap they'd been investigating.

Her stomach churned more each day with the unanswered questions and the knowledge that more girls were being taken advantage of the longer they took to make arrests.

Sean waited downstairs on the front porch since his presence had freaked Katie out. She'd spent the first ten minutes hysterical, convinced they were going to arrest her, so ultimately they thought it would be better if Sean waited outside. He'd retrieved his laptop and used a wireless connection to contact some friends about unsending Katie's e-mail before her boyfriend opened the photos.

Now, Donata hoped they could wrap up this night of tears and self-recrimination so she could deliver Katie to her father. And once the girl was safe, Donata planned to track down Katie's boyfriend for a little conversation unless Mick insisted on taking that privilege himself. Katie's story of high pressure from her boyfriend—right down to insisting on a certain file size for the pictures—made Donata suspect an organized business was recruiting teenage boys to obtain at least some of the illicit footage for them.

That was one solid lead, at least.

"My friend is doing everything in his power to retrieve the photos from Trevor's e-mail." Donata touched Katie's shoulder, surprised at how fragile she seemed even though her father was such a big guy. "And it's inviting trouble to hang out in a house like this where ten different guys probably have keys to the place."

"You think my judgment sucks where guys are concerned, don't you?" Katie looked up at her with big brown eyes, the girl's thick dark hair knotted in an intricate ponytail with ten different clips holding back stray pieces.

"I think my judgment about guys sucked when I was your age, let's put it that way." She knew it was better now. Just thinking about Sean made her feel stronger. And shouldn't a woman be with a man who made her feel better about herself instead of a guy who dragged her down? Not that self-worth should be attached a man, but sheesh. "You might be infinitely smarter than me, yet I can't help but look back and think how much I wanted to be the center of some guy's world when I was fifteen. I know how that kind of thinking puts a girl at a distinct disadvantage."

"But I don't need to be the center of someone's world. I just wanted to be the hot chick around school instead of the new girl for a change." She shrugged, her simple self-awareness making Donata think the girl would be okay. And since Donata had the boyfriend's name and contact information in her jacket pocket she figured her work here was done.

She handed Katie her purse just as a shot fired outside the house.

Glass broke in response to the shot, a thousand little pieces showering to a floor somewhere inside the apartment building.

Sean.

"Get down." Donata yanked Katie to the floor of the apartment and rolled her under a table. "Stay down. Call your father."

Heart slamming into her throat, Donata pulled her cell out of her jacket and handed it to the girl before she scuttled toward the door, remaining beneath window level.

"Where are you going?" Katie screeched, her voice thready with panic.

"To make sure no one gets hurt." She'd never forgive herself if she ignored all Sean's warnings that this might be a setup only to have him on the wrong end of a bullet.

Oh God.

A wave of sickness roiled but before she lost it, Sean's voice shouted up from outside.

"Donata?" He sounded strong. Whole.

Thank you, God. She'd never guessed detective work would make her so nauseous, but having Sean involved in this with her added a whole new dimension of fears she didn't want to analyze right now.

"I'm here. We're okay." She was amazed to realize that in her three years on the street as a beat cop, she'd never had cause to draw her weapon. The last time she'd held a gun outside of the practice range had been in that final showdown with Sergio.

"I'm on the line with local police now. I can see the window that took the bullet and it was definitely fired from outside so you should be fine if you stay put and stay low. No sign of anyone out here."

Stay put while Sean remained outside with someone firing shots at the house?

Not bloody likely.

Donata had made a lot of mistakes in her life, but taking the easy way out wasn't one of them. And after making sure Katie was safely wedged beneath a table with her cell phone in hand, Donata started down the stairs of the house to help Sean fight their unseen foe.

TWO HOURS OF SEARCHING the neighborhood brought them another dead end in an investigation that went nowhere. For every step forward they took two back and the frustration threatened to unravel inside him after tonight's near miss by a perp they couldn't pinpoint. After he and Donata had both given statements and Mick had arrived to personally escort his shaken daughter home, Sean drove Donata away from Long Beach.

His head was buzzing with "what ifs" after a close call. The bullet they'd found had been one floor below where Donata and Katie had been talking.

Judging by the buzz around the crime scene, either Katie or Donata would be dead now if the shooter had aimed slightly higher.

And wasn't that a sobering-as-hell realization?

"I can't drive all the way back to the city." He pulled off the highway without consulting her, needing to touch her more than he needed her approval or even her understanding right now.

"What are you doing?" She straightened in her seat, eyes darting over to the speedometer as he braked hard to get off the interstate.

"Pulling over. Getting a room somewhere. I don't know." His whole body hurt with the effort to rein himself in lately, the effort to be patient and methodical on a case he'd long approached from gut instinct.

Holding back now to wait for ballistics reports and political maneuvering between police departments on crimes that reached far outside Manhattan wore his patience thin. Add to that the need to be with Donata, to wrap her in his arms and bury himself inside her after those moments of gut-wrenching fear following the gunfire and it was no wonder he was going crazy.

She could have died back there.

"We could be home in twenty minutes," she reminded him, looking both ways as he sped through a yellow light.

"That's twenty minutes too long." He didn't have the energy or brainpower left to explain himself at this point. He only knew he needed to touch her, to reassure himself she'd come through unscathed.

He pulled into the parking lot of a coffee shop when no hotels were immediately visible.

"What are we—"

"It's just for a minute." He wheeled the vehicle around to the back of the place and parked under a tree.

No streetlights back here. Just the backs of three other concrete buildings and a tree that refused to bow to the urban sprawl.

Shoving the gearshift into park, he switched off the ignition and had both their seat belts off in a matter of seconds. Only another second or two to push his seat all the way back and pull Donata across the vehicle into his lap.

Her eyes were wide with surprise until he started unbuttoning her blouse. Then, seeming to understand, her lids went heavy.

He speared a hand into her hair, cradling the back of her head with his palm. Holding her steady he kissed her, popping one button after another with his other hand.

The scent of her perfume rose from her breasts as he unveiled them. Even after a full workday, hours at the computer and a trip to Long Beach, the scent of her floral fragrance lingered, intensified by the heat of her skin.

The temperature spiked in the vehicle as fog spread across the windows and clouded them in privacy. Private by his standards anyway.

"I need you. I need to hold you, feel your body pulsing and alive around me." He'd meant to ask her if she minded being here, getting naked in a coffee shop parking lot. But the words morphed into something else without his consent.

And damn it, he did need her. He needed to know that some stupid criminal's bullet hadn't landed her on a morgue slab, cold and lifeless and out of his world forever. A thought beyond contemplating.

He pulled her to him a little rougher than he intended, but she didn't object. In fact, she seemed to echo his sentiments with nails scoring his back.

"Amen." She barely moved her lips off his to speak the word, but Sean heard the assent in her voice and felt it in the slow roll of her hips against his.

Past the point of finesse, he leaned back to give her more room to wriggle out of her jeans. The blue denim went sailing into the back seat along with the hint of black lace she'd been wearing underneath.

How could she wear such blatantly provocative lingerie beneath her clothes all the time and not drive him totally insane? He could never concentrate on work with her around no matter how conservatively she dressed because he knew that a sexpot lurked behind the detached facade.

He had his fly undone and a condom on by the time she was undressed, but then he didn't have to perform half the acrobatics she did for sexual access. Her blouse still fluttered open, her breasts half falling out of her bra from when he'd started working at the front hook.

"I want you all the time." He lifted her at the waist, raising her up enough to find his way inside her, positioning himself right there for one suspended moment until he brought her down in one long stroke.

Fireworks started behind his eyeballs even though his eyes were wide open. Her hair fell in a silky stroke across his arm as she leaned over him, her breath coming in short pants as she worked her hips faster.

If they'd had more room he would have made her wait, could have exerted his own will in this encounter because he didn't want it to end. But he'd gotten to have her here, now, in the front seat of his vehicle in a parking lot.

And holy hell, how lucky was that? He figured he owed it to her to let her call the shots on how this encounter went down. He just needed to feel her around him, warm and alive and incredible.

Her hips still gyrating in ways that made his eyes cross, Donata arched in a way that dragged her breasts slowly across his chest. The combination of the quick hip action and the lush stroke of her full breasts sent the sexual fireworks into a mind-blowing finale, his fingers sinking into her hips as he held her tight to him.

I love you.

Sean thought the words even if he didn't speak them aloud. He didn't know that he was the kind of guy who even knew how to say them anymore, but just thinking them blew his mind.

He couldn't speak the words now anyway since she'd think it was the sex talking. And even though the sex had been incredible enough to induce babbling in a grown man, Sean knew that he'd feel the same way tomorrow. How scary was that? He'd avoided relationships for years. Then Donata walked back into his life and after a handful of days together—bam! He suddenly couldn't get enough of this woman.

Those tense moments back in Long Beach when he thought she might have been hit had crystallized his feelings for her in an instant. But did she think about him the same way?

He knew better than to talk to her about any of this now when they'd been through so much already today and they had to question Richie Ford first thing in the morning.

So it surprised him when she eased off him to start regrouping, her movements stilted and abrupt.

"Donata?" He thought something seemed off.

Maybe she wasn't a fan of car sex.

But then she looked back at him with a steely determination in her blue eyes and he knew it didn't have anything to do with sex.

"I'm sorry. But we can't keep doing this, Sean."

15

FINGERS FLYING over the buttons on her blouse, Donata wondered why she couldn't make smarter decisions in her life. This had probably been a really stupid time to have such a discussion and her tenuous grip on her emotions loosened every time she got next to Sean lately.

"What do you mean?" He watched her from the driver's seat that he'd returned to a sitting position.

His rumpled hair and sweat-sheened skin only made him all the more enticing as he pulled his clothes into place. He moved with slow deliberation while she scuttled all over the car to retrieve her things.

"I mean I can't mix work and pleasure anymore because it's frying my ability to think." And it was even more than mixing work and her personal life since this aspect of personal life scared the crap out of her. She'd given her whole life over to Sergio and what she was feeling now for Sean totally overshadowed anything she'd ever felt for Sergio. What if she lost herself altogether?

How could she keep her identity in the midst of such all-encompassing emotion?

Besides, Sean's life had been at stake tonight. And wasn't that reason enough to slow things down?

"Donata." Sean looked at her as if she'd lost her mind. He held both her hands that couldn't keep still.

But she shook off his touch and whatever his words might have been in a rush to share all the ways she was freaking out.

"No. Listen. Beyond the fact that you could have died tonight because I ignored your instincts to call for backup, I also happen to have a whole career riding on my talk with Richie Ford tomorrow and I don't even have the first clue what to ask or how to handle the encounter. Do you realize the stakes for messing this up? I could lose out on an arrest. I could be responsible for keeping a predator on the streets."

Not to mention she could lose her job.

She'd sound horribly selfish to reiterate that fact, and it truly ranked lower on her list of priorities in light of her feelings for Sean. But the truth of the matter was that she'd crossed out of the criminal world recently enough that she highly valued the one and only legitimate job she'd ever done. What would she have if she failed as a detective?

"So you can't mix work and pleasure." He repeated her words as he turned on the defogger to clear the steamy windows. "And you're choosing work."

At no small cost to her heart.

"For now. I don't have a choice if I'm going to pull my weight on this case." She had to be sharp even if she didn't feel it.

Sean didn't say anything as he studied the small spot on the window the defogger cleared. The spot spread bigger and bigger until the windshield was clear everywhere except a thin strip along the top of the glass.

"This case is important to you." He nodded as though it made sense to him, yet the hard set to his features told her he didn't understand at all.

She wasn't so sure she understood herself. But her life was a work in progress and this next phase was supposed to be about finding professional security and maybe, just maybe, peace with her past.

"I can't afford to mess up this case, Sean. It's the most extensive investigation I've been a part of and I've played a larger role in this one than anything I've done before."

"You don't have to explain." He leaned over the console and kissed her on the cheek with a tenderness that made her heart stutter. "I know you've worked damn hard to be a detective. You're going to knock the nay-saying buttheads on their asses when you make the arrests on this one."

He put the vehicle in reverse and drove away from the place where they'd made love. And although he'd done exactly what she wanted, Donata definitely didn't feel happy about it.

"YOU BROKE UP with the guy?" Mick glanced at her over the rim of his coffee mug as they turned off F.D.R. Drive on their way to Richie Ford's place on the Lower East Side.

They had a search warrant based on the information from Sergio and Richie's alias connection to fastgirlz, so Donata felt calmer about the meeting than she had the night before. Well, she felt calmer about work. She grew more tense by the hour as she thought about how things had grown stilted and awkward between her and Sean by the end of the night. Actually, it had been almost daybreak by the time he walked her into her apartment.

Her heart had started hurting the second he walked out of her place.

"We didn't exactly break up. We hadn't ever officially dated in the first place." She felt a little better when she remembered that. And he had gone out of his way to make it clear he'd never committed to anything long term.

"Things looked fairly intense between you last night for a couple who never dated." Mick settled the mug into a cup holder on the console and Donata guessed his tired eyes were held open by the miracle of caffeine alone.

"We'd been shot at," Donata argued, remembering the way Sean seemed to touch her continuously after their backup had arrived to escort Katie out of the building. "That's intense by itself."

"I've been shot at a time or two and I don't remember ever palming my partner's butt. Although your butt is a lot better than the last guy's." He grinned as he downshifted for a stop light.

Commuters poured across the crosswalk in a human flood even though they were still many blocks from the busy financial district. Everyone had somewhere to go at 9:00 a.m., apparently, even in a neighborhood turned trendy in recent years despite its old rep for drug dealers and rent-controlled apartments. There was the mix of change here and, as usual, the artists and musicians, designers and restaurateurs were the urban pioneers to start the revolution.

"I think you're mistaken about the butt palming. Although I get your point. We didn't need to have dated to be close."

And they *had* gotten close.

Her throat tightened to think she'd made a panicky mistake because Sean made her feel things she wasn't ready to feel again.

"All I'm saying is that it seems a little hasty when you've been working together for what? A week or so?"

Is that all it had been? The days had blurred when their nights were spent in a police station or in the middle of a crime scene. And the other nights had been far more wonderful but equally tiring since they hadn't involved sleep.

"I just needed some space until this investigation

closes." Her eyes burned thinking she messed up something good. Something rare.

"You might want to make sure he understands you were only angling for some time. I don't know Beringer all that well, but some guys might take offense at being given the boot in the middle of a tense investigation, when people aren't at their best anyway. He's been developing this bust for a long time."

Was she so insensitive that she needed a *guy* to tell her how clueless she was being? She should have talked things through more with Sean. Except that the strength of the passion had blown her away and she could barely string two words together the night before. By the time they were through, she'd been so vulnerable that she protected herself the only way she knew how.

She'd given herself some space.

But now, it seemed, she might have more space than she could handle.

"This is it." Mick's voice dragged her back to their morning mission at Richie's house. Another car of officers—including two with computer expertise—waited at the end of the block. The driver of the other vehicle waved to Mick as they rolled past. Scents of ethnic foods—Vietnamese cooking or Thai, maybe—drifted right through the windows even though the only businesses Donata spotted were a few bars and a music store.

This was why she'd asked Sean for space, right? So she could approach days like this with more clear-headed focus. Too bad she sat outside an important suspect's house, search warrant at the ready, thinking about her screwed-up personal life instead of work.

"Are you ready?" Mick had already switched off the car. He patted his pocket to be sure he had the warrant.

"The sooner we make an arrest, the sooner life can get back to normal." Or so she sincerely hoped. "Let's go."

Mick put his hand on her arm.

"If this is the guy behind the break-ins at your apartment and the bed-and-breakfast, you need to be careful today. Whoever rigged those computers has it in for you."

"I'm always careful." Probably too careful when it came to Sean, damn it. But at least in her work environment, caution paid off.

A minute later they were out of the car and on Delancey Street with their team behind them to execute the search of the premises. Donata and Mick walked shoulder to shoulder as they moved past the yawning doorman and up the stairs to the second-floor apartment. For a moment, she felt a small thrill at the possibility of her first big bust. Despite the danger, despite being shot at the night before and awake almost until dawn, Donata couldn't suppress the sense of rightness surging through her with each step toward Richie Ford's door.

When they arrived on his welcome mat, she rang the bell and waited, wishing she could recount this moment for Sean later. If he was still speaking to her.

A knot of trepidation settled in her stomach, worsened by the scent of scorched eggs from an apartment nearby. The knot only tightened when the person who answered the door wasn't Richie Ford.

The woman on the other side of threshold had a face Donata had prayed never to see again. Rosario Gillespie. *Dear, sweet Rosie.*

The tall brunette with killer curves and a loud mouth had been Sergio's mistress back when Donata still cared. She stood in Richie's apartment now with a purse under one arm and a fur-trimmed wool coat draped around her shoulders like a cape.

Donata was so stunned she forgot to announce their reason for being there. Rosie took the opportunity to get the ball rolling as she cackled her Wicked Witch of the West laugh.

"Jesus H. Christ, Donata, you look like hell. But then I suppose your beauty budget isn't what it used to be now that Serg is in jail?"

Mick flashed the warrant in Rosie's face while Donata tried to scoop her jaw off the ground at seeing the woman Serg said had moved to the country.

Rosie peered at the paper and then back at Mick.

"I'm afraid your little note doesn't include searching me since I don't live here." She twitched her hips in obvious display, lips puckered into an air kiss. "Better luck next time, detectives."

She strolled past them out of apartment 2A and Donata thanked God for small favors. That is, until she saw the Wicked Bitch of the West pause in the hallway to talk to a man leaning against a supply closet door. A man with an all-too familiar silhouette.

Sean.

Her brief flutter of excitement was quickly squelched by the realization that the two of them were chatting like long-lost friends. Apparently they knew one another. Well.

Doing her best to ignore an unreasonable explosion of jealousy, Donata turned on her heel and entered Richie's apartment.

IF SEAN HADN'T already been suffering a bad case of heartbreak, he might have been offended at the death-ray glare Donata had just given him.

As it was, he needed to put personal feelings aside since the pivotal point in Donata's case was already walking away, possibly with a boatload of evidence stashed in that oversize purse of hers.

He dashed into the apartment to see Mick arguing with a man Sean recognized as their suspect while the search team moved with quick efficiency around the rooms. Donata stood off to one side of the living room, staring at the titles of books and CDs on the shelves of a shiny chrome media cabinet.

"We've got to go." Sean reached for her, arm snaking around her waist in a gesture that had become so easy, so automatic.

Damn it.

"I'm in the middle of conducting a search." Her eyebrows rose high in surprise then narrowed in condemnation. "I can't leave now."

Sean gestured to Mick, knowing he had enough years on the force to appreciate that breaks in a case could happen at any time. Even in the middle of a search.

Donata played by the book because she was new to the field, but one day… Sean could see her running the whole outfit once she had the experience to go with her cool head and natural skills as an investigator. He just wished he'd have a front row view to see that happen instead of being banished from her life.

"Your best lead is slipping away." He half pulled her out of the modest apartment in a lackluster building, keeping his voice low so that irate Richie wouldn't notice them leaving and tip off Rosie.

"What are you talking about? I need to be here." She dug in her heels just after they crossed the threshold into the hallway with cracked linoleum tiles from about four decades ago. "This is my job, damn it."

How could he convince her to follow his instincts when he'd been pegged as the loose cannon for so many years?

"I know Rosie and I know she's trouble. I contacted her way back when my sister was molested because Rosie had some photos of herself in circulation at that same time and I thought she might need help to get out of a bad situation."

Donata glanced back into the apartment—toward Mick—for only a moment and then seemed to make a decision.

"I can walk and listen."

Sean led her toward the back stairwell he'd come up earlier when he'd decided to be a presence at Richie Ford's today. Just because Donata didn't want anything more to do with him didn't mean he'd turn his back on a case he'd worked his butt off to solve.

"Hurry. She's wearing four-inch heels so we'll be faster, but she got a jump start on us and she might have a car out front."

They tore down the service entry stairs, the sound of their pounding feet echoing too loudly in the bare stairwell for Sean to finish his story. The scent of garbage and urine hung heavy in the air even though there were no obvious signs of trash. The place was just old.

And damn but it felt right to have her at his side, working with him. Being together. How could this sense of connection he felt be so one-sided? His gut felt hollow. Empty.

"There she is." Donata pointed down the street where Rosie was just rounding a corner. "Mick's car is parked down there but I don't have keys."

"If she didn't call for a cab from that corner, maybe her destination doesn't require a ride." He took off running down the block, surprised at how well Donata kept up despite his longer legs.

And why did he have to keep finding things to admire about her?

Reaching the corner of Forsyth Street, they skidded to a stop. Rosie was sauntering into a building that looked more commercial than residential with no awning, no obvious building number and a UPS delivery truck double-parked out front.

"Want me to find a back entrance?" Donata stood at his side, assessing the situation.

"No. Let's stick together and hope she's not planning to bolt. I don't think she knows we're behind her."

"Why do *you* think she's hiding something?" Donata asked as they closed in on the building.

"When I contacted her four years ago to see if she needed help, she had a mercenary take on the whole industry." He raised his voice as a street sweeper went by. "Her words were something like 'if I can make money off a bunch of pervs with no self-control, why shouldn't I?'"

Donata said nothing as they reached the building. The door was—happily—unlocked.

"Why do you think she's hiding something?" He returned the question hoping maybe Donata simply trusted him.

"She hates my guts. She was Sergio's other woman before we broke up. I couldn't imagine who would want to stalk me personally with Sergio in jail, but I suppose she fits the bill, even if she did wait a hell of a long time to take revenge."

"You think she'd post naked pictures of you to get even?" He looked around the long corridor of doors and realized they'd lost Rosie.

"Four years ago she hated me enough to strap me down naked in a patch of fire ants if she had the opportunity. I thought maybe she would have moved on after Serg went to jail, but some people hang onto anger more than others, apparently." Donata peered in a door on one side of the hallway while he tried to crack open a locked door on the other.

Donata moved to the next door on her side while Sean pulled a slim metal pick out of his pocket. Since he didn't believe in letting a locked door stop him, he carried a simple lock-picking device on his key ring. He worked the lock while Donata worked her way farther down the hall, checking in other doors.

"Since she obviously knows a thing or two about computers if she's hanging out with Richie Ford, I'd say it's a safe bet she wouldn't think twice about rigging your home computer." The lock slid open and Sean peered inside a dark room full of stacked black containers…DVD cases?

Hot damn.

"I think we may have hit pay dirt here."

When she didn't answer he moved out into the hallway.

"Donata?"

Only silence answered the call. Guilt mixed with

fear and the certainty that he'd screwed up. His gut sank as he called her again.

But he knew she wouldn't answer because he already suspected what had happened. He'd turned his head for minute and just like that—

She was gone.

16

DOWN THE HALL, Donata listened for Sean from the steely imprisonment of a thug's smelly arms. She hadn't meant to get ahead of Sean when she stepped into a partially open door not quite halfway down the long corridor of the building that looked to be a half-abandoned storage facility. She'd just been focused on moving swiftly so they wouldn't lose Rosie the Tart-turned-Criminal.

But then two guys had grabbed her with the quick efficiency of professional muscle. Their combined efforts enabled them to clamp her mouth shut while stripping her of her gun and immobilizing her against a brick wall covered in cobwebs. Her cheek scraped the stony face of the brick as one of the bouncer-size guys kept his hand clamped over her mouth. She was no slouch in the fighting department either, having learned at a young age she could compensate for her lack of size and modest strength with guts, determination and dirty moves. But there was no room for kneeing anyone in the balls or gouging an eyeball. These guys were just that good.

Her cheek bled now while she was being shoved down the hall, farther away from Sean. The warm stream trickled down into her mouth, coating her lips with a metallic tinge.

"Donata?" Sean's voice shouted from the corridor, his footsteps running closer over worn linoleum.

Was anyone else lying in wait for him? Her heart pounded with the need to warn him but she could barely move a muscle on her own with the might of Hans and Franz suffocating her whole body.

"Quickly," a woman's voice came from nearby, the clammy-smelling room too dark to distinguish exactly where.

Donata guessed it was Rosie telling her two steroid-inflated freaks to get the lead out. Donata tried dragging her feet or flailing her arms, anything to make some noise that would tell Sean what room she was in. But she was carried to the other side of the room with such precision manhandling—woman handling?—she wasn't able to make a sound. Her muffled grunts wouldn't carry more than five feet.

"Donata?" Sean's voice sounded farther away this time and she realized at the same time that she was being dragged out of the building into a closed space that smelled like a basement.

No. A garage.

Even in the dim light of an overcast day filtering through a high window and the fiberglass overhead door, she could see the outline of a white delivery van on the other side of a wall of boxes. Hans and Franz seemed to home in on the van.

They were moving her. Transporting her off-site.

That could *not* happen.

People died when they were moved to another location. And if anything happened to her…Sean would never quit his campaign to punish the people responsible. He'd ignore his P.I. business and turn away new clients. He'd be the king of short term forever if she didn't convince him they were perfect for each other because they were both such chicken-shits when it came to risking a relationship.

She struggled harder against her captor, finally breaking an arm free enough to scrape her fingernails along the cement block wall as she sought vainly for any kind of leverage.

Nails breaking in record speed, Donata knew her options were fiercely limited by the stranglehold the Rambo-wannabe had her in so she tried the only other ploy she could think of. She tightened every muscle in her body and strained mightily against the guy. She knew she'd never make him so much as crack a sweat, but her movement forced him to readjust his hold on her before he could toss her in the back of the van.

And once he positioned himself to account for her struggles, Donata switched tactics and went as bone-less as she could, slumping down heavily to wiggle out of his arms like gelatin. Thank God for the man's nylon jacket. She slid down him like a greased cat.

As his arm loosened and the guy swore, his hand came away from her mouth long enough for her to shout out to Sean.

"In the garage! Help!" Her shrill words bounced all around the cement walls and up to the rafters. With any luck, people on the street would hear her through the fiberglass door, too.

Of course, she hadn't counted on the wrath of Rosie. Donata couldn't even formulate the next step of her plan when she saw Rosie's hand coming toward her with a gun pressed into her palm.

Donata barely thought "pistol whip" before her head jerked back on contact and her thoughts turned off completely.

GARAGE?

Where the hell was the garage?

Sean raced through one room after another until he spotted a back entrance in a brick-lined storage space full of boxes on one side. Tearing through the shadows and cobwebs, he followed the remembered sound of her voice in the eerie silence that followed.

If they'd hurt her to shut her up…

Sean made bargains with God as he pushed through the door and found himself facing a white delivery van roaring to life. Was Donata inside? He prayed they were taking her somewhere and that they hadn't simply left her for dead in a dark corner of the cluttered loading area.

The van squealed its way into Reverse, bashing

into the closed garage door. He shot the front tire and would have fired into the driver's area if only he could be one hundred percent certain Donata wasn't up front.

He wrenched open the passenger side door of the incapacitated van and jammed his gun into the gut of the ape-size man who tried to leap out. The man who'd been driving raised his arms in surrender.

Smart bastard. Sean was about a heartbeat away from firing on them if they didn't show him a healthy—whole—Donata soon.

"Hold it," a feminine voice screeched out into the echoing garage of concrete walls and metal rafters.

Sean waited, still holding his gun on Neanderthal man as Rosario Gillespie stepped out of the side door of the van, her tall figure hiding anything behind her.

Could Donata be inside? They would have had to tie her up to keep her from fighting back. Or incapacitate her some other way.

Rage and fear mixed into a deadly emotion.

"Where the hell is Donata?" His finger itched on the trigger, anger firing through him red-hot and lethal.

"She'll be dead in ten more seconds if you don't let go of him." She gestured with a snub-nosed weapon toward the giant. "Release him now."

That was the last thing he wanted to do with no assurances they hadn't hurt her. Or worse.

The thought leveled him.

"Show her to me." He didn't know if someone might be holding a gun to her inside the van and he wouldn't risk pissing off this woman just in case.

"She's being held inside by a man I wouldn't want to upset if I were you." Rosie reached down beside her, her weapon still trained on Sean, and came up with a brown leather shoe.

Donata's shoe.

Something went haywire inside him—the old unpredictability that had gotten him in so much trouble on the job as a cop. He fought the darkness inside, however, knowing he didn't have a prayer of saving Donata if he didn't keep his cool.

"How do I know she's not dead?" The word reverberated around his brain with devastating volume, but he asked the question with such quiet coolness he almost couldn't believe it had been his voice.

Inside he wanted to strangle this woman—slowly—with both hands. But if Donata was inside the van being held by someone he couldn't see, he had to give her time to do her job.

"I guess you don't know for sure. But really, why risk her life by doubting me?" Rosie smiled archly, ignoring the hubbub of voices out on the street as people gathered around the dented garage door to see what was going on.

The people on the street couldn't see in, but their shadows through the heavy fiberglass were a strange presence in the drama inside the garage. The man Sean held at gunpoint sweated profusely, his fear a palpable smell.

He knew as well as Sean did that someone would call the cops and this little drama would be over soon. But would Rosie lay off her trigger finger long enough to ensure they all remained in one piece?

"Why would I kill her when I could publicly humiliate her for as long as I like?" Rosie shook her head as if he'd asked a stupid question. "Donata painted me as a homewrecking slut to Sergio's friends back when I had no idea the guy was even involved with anyone else. And by the time I realized the truth, why would I just roll over and let the bitch have him when Sergio was clearly bored with her?"

Color suffused Rosie's cheeks, her dark hair tumbling wildly around her shoulders as she kept her focus on Sean and her hand steady.

"So you've been using Sergio's old pictures of Donata to embarrass her?" His eyes were adjusting to the darkened garage, waiting for some sign of movement within the van.

Some sign of her.

Please, God, let her be okay. He couldn't let himself think about the alternative.

"I thought I'd help her lose her job the way she made me lose Sergio."

"You mean you lost your gravy train. What the hell do you care about Sergio?"

"I cared plenty," Rosie shouted back, wobbling on her high heels as she leaned forward to stress the point. She had the crazy-eyed look of a woman scorned who'd gone off the deep end.

"Did you know Donata went to see him at the prison? Sergio has her on his list of visitors he wants to see." The fact had pissed off Sean even if he hadn't cared to admit it, but it was nothing but a pleasure to throw it in this woman's face now.

She paled and then—suddenly—went flying forward as two hands reached from inside the van and shoved Rosie face-first toward the pavement.

Rosie's gun went off as she fell and Sean pushed the big guy to the ground to make sure he didn't run. Sean needn't have worried since both of the hired muscle guys lay obediently on the floor while he covered them with his weapon.

"Everybody remain down," Donata called from within the van. She stepped out of the darkened interior and into the scant light of the garage.

Keeping one foot planted on Rosie's back, Donata met Sean's gaze in time for him to see her bloodied face. Fury simmered at the sight.

"Holy shit." His knees damn near buckled at the sight of her and he wished he could hold her even knowing this wasn't the time.

"Could you kindly ask Rambo for my service revolver before I'm forced to kick his ass, too?" Donata's words were feisty and strong, the take-no-crap tones of a woman who would never admit defeat.

Sean's heart damn near cracked wide open, the swell of love for her so big he could scarcely contain it. He didn't know how he'd ever walk away from this incredible woman who didn't want him in her life anymore.

"Yes, ma'am." He pushed the nose of his weapon harder into the guy's side. "Keep your hands where I can see them pal, and tell me where I can find the lady's gun."

The driver of the van, who was still sprawled across the front of the bench seat, croaked out something about the glove compartment and Sean retrieved the weapon.

"Excellent." Donata took the weapon and kept it trained on Rosie while she pocketed the other woman's fallen gun. "Now why don't we head over to the precinct and you all can explain to us exactly what role you played in creating smut tapes of unsuspecting teenagers while I book you for assault on a police officer."

She swiped at a trail of blood on her neck, her one eye already swollen and purple.

"I didn't—" Rosie began to say.

"Save it," Donata told her, putting her fallen shoe on her one bare foot. "You're gonna look like hell in one of those orange jumpsuits, you know that?"

17

"DO YOU WANT to come upstairs?" Donata stood outside the door to her building after Sean dropped her off at her apartment that evening.

The paperwork had been filed at the precinct and Rosie had admitted her deep hatred for Donata, even if she hadn't confessed on all the charges against her and her new boyfriend, Richie Ford. Thankfully, Mick had brought in Richie earlier that day along with the guy's computer files that incriminated him as an online predator who offered big bucks to teenage boys to plant webcams on the computers of their female acquaintances. The scam had yielded lots of juicy footage for Ford and his girlfriend to post on their private, subscription-only Web site that had morphed out of the original "fastgirlz" site.

Sean opened the door for her, but his feet didn't venture across the threshold.

"You don't know how much I'd like that, Donata, but I don't think that would be wise considering your need to cool things off between us."

The day had already challenged Donata to the

limit as a professional. The cut on her cheek still burned and her eye had swollen purple beneath her eyebrow. But the challenge confronting her now had the potential to hurt her more deeply than any physical wound.

"I'm sorry I panicked in the car. I don't think I expressed myself very well and I wish you'd at least let me explain." She didn't pay any attention to the pedestrian traffic on the street behind her as she stood outside the open door. Inside her building a young couple exchanged kisses and curious looks as they checked their mailbox. But all Donata cared about was fixing things with Sean.

A grizzled older man walking his dog entered the building as Sean held open the door. Even the furry white pooch rubbing against Donata's leg didn't distract her from maintaining eye contact with Sean since she had the feeling if she let him go now, it would be another four years before their paths crossed again.

"Whether you expressed it well or not, I definitely got the message." Sean reached for her cheek on the uninjured side of her face and brushed a gentle thumb over her jaw. "Being alone with you hurts too much."

Had she already chased him away for good with her need to protect her heart? The thought sent a pang through her core, assuring her she'd failed miserably on that count.

"You know, in my old relationship, I would have

just faked that my vision was blurry to get help up the stairs and land the object of my affection right where I wanted." She recalled the way she and Sergio had worked around each other to fulfill their needs and pretend they had a good rapport. "But I don't want to play games with you, Sean, because I respect you too much for that. I made a mistake and I really, really need you to come upstairs for five minutes. If you want to leave after that and continue your reign as the king of short term, I promise I'll understand."

She gladly shed her pride—one quality that usually never failed her—to gamble on a man worth so much more than her facade as a tough chick.

At his small nod, he dropped his hand from her face and Donata walked inside the building. As he followed her into the elevator and down her hall, she knew she needed to find the right words to make him stay. To make him understand she wasn't the kind of woman to change her mind every other day.

"Will you continue to investigate this case now that you've arrested two of the primary suspects?" He switched the topic to business, and she wondered if that was to deflect the serious tone of an intimate conversation or because he wanted to retreat into the comfort of his professional world.

"You don't think we'll find out that Richie and Rosie have been turning the webcam footage into mass-marketed films?" The pair had so many DVDs stockpiled in the warehouse that Donata had hoped a little more police work would link the twosome to the larger distribution scheme that put the webcam footage on store shelves as reality porn.

Sean shook his head as she unlocked her apartment door and let them inside.

"The footage they sell by the private subscription Web site is too raw and unpolished compared to the slick product that goes into movie rental places and stores. The packaging of those pieces is done by someone with more film industry savvy and the connections to distribute underage porn without any red flags."

"You think Rosie is in cahoots with some Hollywood type?" Donata found it hard to believe any legitimate industry professional would have anything to do with a woman who practically seethed evil. Rosie had been behind all of the personal attacks on Donata's privacy. The woman's jealousy and resentment had only grown in the last four years. Sergio's former mistress had even been the one to take a sniper shot from a neighboring building the night before since she'd been following Donata all week. That alone would amount to serious jail time.

"Not necessarily. But this could be the work of an underling in a New York production company. There are certainly plenty of filmmakers in the city with the clout to get their movies on store shelves throughout the country."

"I don't know if I'll continue working the case." Donata tossed her keys on her coffee table and slipped out of her shoes. "Although if you want to keep tracking that angle, I'd work with you if you'd have me."

Truth be told, the teen exploitation angle was a little too close to home for her comfort and she felt as though she'd done a good deed by bringing Rosie in. But if it meant salvaging at least *some* kind of relationship with Sean, Donata would continue her efforts on the reality porn case.

He slid his jacket off his shoulders in the first sign that maybe he wouldn't run right out her door and Donata's heart leaped with hope.

"Actually, I think it's time for me to take a little time off from Internet predators. My sister's been asking me to change focus for a while and maybe she's right. I've got a great team of technical people who can track a lot of other online crimes. And now I can say I did my best to blast some of these molesters out of cyber hiding."

"We'll be arresting subscribers to the Web site for the next few weeks." Donata looked forward to that part. "The number of arrests will only go up."

"Making you look damn good in the department's eyes." Sean reached for her, then caught himself midway and shoved his hands in his pockets.

Donata ached with the loss of that touch.

"You're looking damn good as far as the precinct is concerned, too," she said. "You know you could have a place on the detective squad again if you wanted it." She'd seen firsthand that his techniques—while sometimes unconventional—were effective.

"I don't. I'm happier calling the shots for myself. My instincts might not always be on the money, but they serve me well."

Seeing an opening, she took a deep breath.

"My instincts aren't always the best either. That's why I ended up blurting out a plea for space that I really don't want after Rosie took a shot at us last night."

Silence met her admission for a long moment.

"I've been so careful with women since my sister was molested because I'd never want to be the pushy guy who took advantage of a date."

"You'd never be that kind of man."

"You thought I was." His eyes broadcast the pain of her long-ago accusation in a way he'd never let her see before. "I'm not blaming you about the accusation, but it made me realize how easily attraction can be misconstrued or even misrepresented. I got even more careful after that."

Her mouthy personality, the one she'd used as a shield during those months of hell she'd lived a lie with Sergio to send him to jail, had ended up hurting this noble, honorable man so much more than she'd realized. Not because of the career he'd walked away from, but because of the guilt she'd heaped on his strong shoulders.

She'd unwittingly played a large role in turning him into the king of short term. Tears burned her eyes as regret singed her heart.

"I'm so sorry." She reached out to him, relieved

when he let her rest her fingertips on his broad shoulder. His chest.

"It's not your fault," he assured her again, even though she knew damn well it was. "That's what happens when your work life focuses on scumbags for so long. Your vision of the world skews and grows more cynical. Darker. I see that now, but I'll never be the kind of guy who can handle a woman who's not one hundred percent sure she knows what she wants."

How could she convince him she wasn't like that when the night before she'd been pushing him away? Her hopes wavered, her fear growing that she'd made her second colossal mistake in her love life. Her first had been falling for a gangster. Would her second be letting the greatest guy she'd ever met slip away?

Her fingers swiped back and forth across his chest, as if she could erase all the mistakes she'd made with him since they'd first met. If only relationships—if only *love*—were that easy.

And she did love him. She knew it today even if she hadn't wanted to face it in the emotional jet lag of the night before. But love didn't disappear just because you were scared to face it. And if anything, she'd awoken today with the knowledge of love in her bones.

"I do know what I want." The resolution in her voice soothed her somehow. Whether Sean recognized it or not, she heard the absolute truth of her words by the strength of her tone.

Twilight cloaked the room in purple hues as a

stray shaft of the sinking sun's rays penetrated her living room window. The light seemed to land on the old photo of her as a girl with her hippie father in the Doors T-shirt, almost as if her misguided but well-meaning dad was encouraging her to be true to herself and not act out her past pattern of self-protection.

Go for it, sweetie.

"I realized I love you last night, Donata." Sean's words were as strong as hers, but tinged with a sadness of a man who knows his love might not be returned. "I'm not in a position to play games or to sleep together. Maybe in the back of my mind I've avoided falling for anyone in the past because I knew when I did, I'd go all out. It's a quirk of personality for me that when I want something, I don't hold back."

His self-deprecating smile gave her the last nudge she needed. This time it would be *her* turn to go all out. Sean wouldn't be the only one taking chances.

"You say you realized you loved me last night after the sniper shot." She cupped his face in her hands, willing him to understand her the way she seemed to understand him. "Well, it only took me a day longer to come to the same conclusion."

His eyebrows furrowed, expression intensifying.

"But you told me you didn't even want us to see each other any more."

"Only because I could feel myself falling down into an abyss of emotion that terrified me and I thought maybe I could stop the descent if I put on the brakes. But I woke up in love with you today, even with the brakes on. I see now that you can't decide to take it slower with someone just because you're scared. Love happens whether or not people feel ready for it."

A grin broke over his face.

"Jesus, lady, you make it sound like a terminal condition."

"No. But it's definitely a permanent one and I can guarantee I'm not going to stop being crazy about you because I'm scared or because you're impulsive when I'd like to study the parameters more." She shook her head, her heart full of things she needed to express. In those moments when she'd realized that Rosie would gladly kill her, Donata had understood she couldn't hold back her feelings for Sean. What if she'd never gotten the chance to tell him how much he meant to her?

Sean's dark gaze raked over her face, searching for answers she would gladly spell out. She closed her eyes and let the words inside her spill free.

"I love that you fight on the right side of the law and I love it that you take the rules into your own hands when it comes to taking skanky pictures of me off the Internet even when I think maybe they need to be there for prosecution purposes. I love that you're willing to share your instincts with me about people like Rosie Gillespie even when I'm only seeing the evidence right in front of my nose. You know how many points I won in the department today because of you?"

Sean studied Donata's face in the soft shadows of evening and knew he'd be powerless to say no to this gutsy, determined lady who had made the best of every single tough situation life had thrown her way. Even now, as she pleaded with him so sweetly, she looked at him through a shiner that would linger on her pretty face for a week or two.

He brushed a thumb across the raw scrape on her cheek and knew he'd risk anything for another shot with her since his every noisy instinct told him she was The One. His first and last long-term woman.

"It wasn't me who won you points with the guys at the precinct." He'd just been doing his job the only way he knew how—following his hunches and making split-second decisions.

"Something made them change their minds about me," she argued, stubborn and maybe just a little bit naive about police politics. But then, she had street smarts in spades to make up for it.

She'd been so focused on building her own character for the past few years that maybe she'd neglected her instinct radar for the people around her.

"You won their admiration by your ability to take a punch. In a police station full of guys, honor is given to those who are willing to spill a little blood for the good of the whole. So when you walk in with an arrest and a black eye to show for it, you buy yourself credibility that no squeaky-clean résumé can provide."

Understanding gleamed in her blue eyes.

"That's sick."

"Sick or not, now you're one of their own."

Her lips pursed in thought.

"But I'd far rather earn your affection than theirs." Her fingertips slid from his face to his chest to twitch restlessly.

"Donata." He tipped his forehead to hers, inhaling the sweet scent of her that lingered despite being dragged through a building and thrown into an old van. "Don't you know you already have my affection?"

"Will you forget about what I said last night?" She gripped his shoulders with surprising strength and Sean heard a world of messages in that urgent touch.

She needed him as badly as he needed her.

The rightness of their being together flowed through him like a warm tide.

"I don't remember anything you said to me last night." He'd gladly fake amnesia on that one.

Her smile clutched at his heart and held tight.

"I love you, Sean."

"I'm right there loving you, too," he whispered, brushing a kiss across her mouth. He cupped her cheek gently in one hand as he drew her closer with the other.

"I hope you brought your pillow tonight," she murmured softly between kisses, her hand skimming under his shirt to splay across his back.

"Yeah?" He tilted her head at a new angle to access all the more of her sweet mouth. "And why is that?"

He knew. But was it so wrong to want to hear her say it?

"I'd like you to spend the night with me. All night. Every night. For as long as you can."

The invitation meant almost as much to him as her saying she loved him since he had a damn good idea how tough it was for Donata to make herself vulnerable to anyone.

"Maybe, if I please you well, you'll let me share your pillow." He'd like nothing better than to please her every way possible if only she'd let him.

Her hips rocked against his as their bodies melded seamlessly together, the heat and fire intensified now that they'd let their hearts come into play. This kind of heat didn't just sizzle. It seared them into true partners. Halves of one stronger whole.

And yeah, that knowledge made it easy for him to cross the line into commitment terrain.

"I'd like that." Her fingers strayed south to the waistband of his jeans. "No stopwatches necessary either."

He could see a future of waking up beside this amazing woman as clearly as he could envision taking her to bed for the rest of his life.

He dipped his head to kiss her neck and taste the soft hollow of flesh beneath her ear.

"Believe me, lady, the pleasure is all mine."

* * * * *

Don't miss the next book in the
NIGHT EYES miniseries!
Be sure to pick up
JUST ONE LOOK
By Joanne Rock
Coming in March 2007
from Harlequin Blaze

Happily ever after is just the beginning...

Turn the page for a sneak preview of
A HEARTBEAT AWAY
by
Eleanor Jones

Harlequin Everlasting—Every great love
has a story to tell. ™
A brand-new series from Harlequin Books

Special? A prickle ran down my neck and my heart started to beat in my ears. Was today really special?

"Tuck in," he ordered.

I turned my attention to the feast that he had spread out on the ground. Thick, home-cooked-ham sandwiches, sausage rolls fresh from the oven and a huge variety of mouthwatering scones and pastries. Hunger pangs took over, and I closed my eyes and bit into soft homemade bread.

When we were finally finished, I lay back against the bluebells with a groan, clutching my stomach.

Daniel laughed. "Your eyes are bigger than your stomach," he told me.

I leaned across to deliver a punch to his arm, but he rolled away, and when my fist met fresh air I collapsed in a fit of giggles before relaxing on my back and staring up into the flawless blue sky. We lay like that for quite a while, Daniel and I, side by side in companionable silence, until he stretched out his hand in an arc that encompassed the whole area.

"Don't you think that this is the most beautiful place in the entire world?"

His voice held a passion that echoed my own feelings, and I rose onto my elbow and picked a buttercup to hide the emotion that clogged my throat.

"Roll over onto your back," I urged, prodding him with my forefinger. He obliged with a broad grin, and I reached across to place the yellow flower beneath his chin.

"Now, let us see if you like butter."

When a yellow light shone on the tanned skin below his jaw, I laughed.

"There…you do."

For an instant our eyes met, and I had the strangest sense that I was drowning in those honey-brown depths. The scent of bluebells engulfed me. A roaring filled my ears, and then, unexpectedly, in one smooth movement Daniel rolled me onto my back and plucked a buttercup of his own.

"And do *you* like butter, Lucy McTavish?" he asked. When he placed the flower against my skin, time stood still.

His long lean body was suspended over mine, pinning me against the grass. Daniel...dear, comfortable, familiar Daniel was suddenly bringing out in me the strangest sensations.

"Do you, Lucy McTavish?" he asked again, his voice low and vibrant.

My eyes flickered toward his, the whisper of a sigh escaped my lips and although a strange lethargy had crept into my limbs, I somehow felt as if all my nerve endings were on fire. He felt it, too—I could see it in his warm brown eyes. And when he lowered his face to mine, it seemed to me the most natural thing in the world.

None of the kisses I had ever experienced could have even begun to prepare me for the feel of Daniel's lips on mine. My entire body floated on a tide of ecstasy that shut out everything but his soft, warm mouth, and I knew that this was what I had been waiting for the whole of my life.

"Oh, Lucy." He pulled away to look into my eyes. "Why haven't we done this before?"

Holding his gaze, I gently touched his cheek, then I curled my fingers through the short thick hair at the base of his skull, overwhelmed by the longing to drown again in the sensations that flooded our bodies. And when his long tanned fingers crept across my tingling skin, I knew I could deny him nothing.

* * * * *

*Be sure to look for A HEARTBEAT AWAY,
available February 27, 2007. And look, too, for
THE DEPTH OF LOVE by Margot Early,
the story of a couple who must learn that love
comes in many guises—and in the end
it's the only thing that counts.*

This February...

Catch NASCAR Superstar **Carl Edwards** *in*

SPEED DATING!

Kendall assesses risk for a living—
so she's the last person you'd
expect to see on the arm of a
race-car driver who thrives on the
unpredictable. But when a bizarre
turn of events—and NASCAR
hotshot Dylan Hargreave—inspire
her to trade in her ever-so-structured
existence for "life in the fast lane"
she starts to feel she might be
on to something!

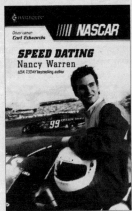

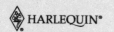
HARLEQUIN®

EVERLASTING LOVE™
Every great love has a story to tell™

Save $1.⁰⁰ off

the purchase of any Harlequin Everlasting Love novel

Coupon valid from January 1, 2007 until April 30, 2007.

Valid at retail outlets in the U.S. only.
Limit one coupon per customer.

5 65373 00076 2 (8100)0 11302

HEUSCPN0407

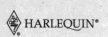

EVERLASTING LOVE™

Every great love has a story to tell™

Save $1.⁰⁰ off

the purchase of
any Harlequin
Everlasting Love novel

Coupon valid from January 1, 2007
until April 30, 2007.

Valid at retail outlets in Canada only.
Limit one coupon per customer.

52607370

HECDNCPN0407

HARLEQUIN® Romance®

From reader-favorite

MARGARET WAY

Cattle Rancher, Convenient Wife

On sale March 2007.

"Margaret Way delivers…
vividly written, dramatic stories."
—*Romantic Times BOOKreviews*

---

*For more wonderful wedding stories,
watch for Patricia Thayer's new miniseries
starting in April 2007.*

Rocky Mountain
BRIDES

REQUEST YOUR FREE BOOKS!

2 FREE NOVELS PLUS 2 FREE GIFTS!

HARLEQUIN®

Blaze.®

Red-hot reads!

YES! Please send me 2 FREE Harlequin® Blaze® novels and my 2 FREE gifts. After receiving them, if I don't wish to receive any more books, I can return the shipping statement marked "cancel." If I don't cancel, I will receive 6 brand-new novels every month and be billed just $3.99 per book in the U.S., or $4.47 per book in Canada, plus 25¢ shipping and handling per book and applicable taxes, if any*. That's a savings of at least 15% off the cover price! I understand that accepting the 2 free books and gifts places me under no obligation to buy anything. I can always return a shipment and cancel at any time. Even if I never buy another book from Harlequin, the two free books and gifts are mine to keep forever.

151 HDN EF3W   351 HDN EF3X

Name	(PLEASE PRINT)
Address	Apt.
City	State/Prov.	Zip/Postal Code

Signature (if under 18, a parent or guardian must sign)

Mail to the Harlequin Reader Service®:
IN U.S.A.: P.O. Box 1867, Buffalo, NY 14240-1867
IN CANADA: P.O. Box 609, Fort Erie, Ontario L2A 5X3

Not valid to current Harlequin Blaze subscribers.

Want to try two free books from another line?
Call 1-800-873-8635 or visit www.morefreebooks.com.

* Terms and prices subject to change without notice. NY residents add applicable sales tax. Canadian residents will be charged applicable provincial taxes and GST. This offer is limited to one order per household. All orders subject to approval. Credit or debit balances in a customer's account(s) may be offset by any other outstanding balance owed by or to the customer. Please allow 4 to 6 weeks for delivery.

Your Privacy: Harlequin is committed to protecting your privacy. Our Privacy Policy is available online at www.eHarlequin.com or upon request from the Reader Service. From time to time we make our lists of customers available to reputable firms who may have a product or service of interest to you. If you would prefer we not share your name and address, please check here. ☐

HB07

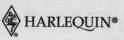

HARLEQUIN®

Blaze™

COMING NEXT MONTH

#309 BEYOND DARING Kathleen O'Reilly
The Red Choo Diaries, Bk. 2
Hot and handsome Jeff Brooks has his hands full "babysitting" his P.R. agency's latest wild-child client, Sheldon Summerville. When she crosses the line, he has no choice but to follow....

#310 A BREATH AWAY Wendy Etherington
The Wrong Bed
Security expert Jade Broussard has one simple rule—never sleep with clients. So why is her latest client, Remy Tremaine, in her bed, sliding his delicious hands all over her? Whatever the reason, she'll toss him out...as soon as she's had enough of those hands!

#311 JUST ONE LOOK Joanne Rock
Night Eyes, Bk. 2
Watching the woman he's supposed to protect take off her clothes is throwing NYPD ballistics expert Warren Vitalis off his game. Instead of focusing on the case at hand, all he can think about is getting Tabitha Everheart's naked self into his bed!

#312 SLOW HAND LUKE Debbi Rawlins
Champion rodeo cowboy Luke McCall claims he's wrongly accused, so he's hiding out. But at a cop's place? Annie Corrigan is one suspicious sergeant, yet has her own secrets. Too bad her wild attraction to her houseguest isn't one of them...

#313 RECKONING Jo Leigh
In Too Deep..., Bk. 3
Delta Force soldier Nate Pratchett is on a mission. He's protecting sexy scientist Tamara Jones while hunting down the bad guys. But sleeping with the vulnerable Tam is distracting him big-time. Especially since he's started battling feelings of love...

#314 TAKE ON ME Sarah Mayberry
Secret Lives of Daytime Divas, Bk. 1
How can Sadie Post be Dylan Anderson's boss when she can't forget the humiliation he caused her on prom night? Worse, her lustful teenage longings for him haven't exactly gone away. There's only one resolution: seduce the man until she's feeling better. *Much* better.

HBCNM0207